NEVER SAY GOODBYE

Ryan turned to me again. "Look, Eden," he said. "I don't want anyone's pity!"

I could barely see his face in the darkened car, but I could see his eyes—frightened, hopeful, hopeless, a little boy's eyes—watching me and pleading with me. I leaned across and kissed him on the lips, gently at first, then not so gently. "Does that feel like pity?" I murmured.

His arms tightened around me. "I want you to be strong," he said. "I need you to be strong, because sometimes I'm scared that I won't be strong enough."

Bantam Sweet Dreams Romances
Ask your bookseller for the books you have missed

Never Say Goodbye

Janet Quin-Harkin

BANTAM BOOKS
TORONTO • NEW YORK • LONDON • SYDNEY • AUCKLAND

RL 6, IL age 12 and up

NEVER SAY GOODBYE
A Bantam Book / April 1988

ISBN 0-553-26702-7

Published simultaneously in the United States and Canada

*Printed and bound in Great Britain by
Hazell Watson & Viney Limited
Member of BPCC plc
Aylesbury Bucks*

Never Say Goodbye

Chapter One

I could smell snow in the wind as I rode to the top of the hill. I knew Charlie could smell it, too, because he threw up his head and stomped nervously.

"It's all right, old boy," I said soothingly, leaning down to pat his rich red flank. "The storm will only be up here in the hills. It won't come down into the valley."

I spurred him on again, to an even walk that was slowed by the cold wind in our faces. "At least it'd better not," I muttered to myself. "It's only October. I'm not ready for winter."

Down below in the valley I could see the school bus, crawling like a fat yellow bug along the ribbon of road. When winter came I would have to ride it again, sitting jammed up with all the other kids while we crawled through the five little townships between the high school and our ranch. Charlie and I could beat the bus home every day, following the old cattle trail along the crest of the hill. Even if we hadn't been able to beat it, riding was a lot better than being squashed in that bus, breathing diesel fumes, listening to loud giggles from the little elementary school kids, and sweating when the heating system was turned on and freezing when it wasn't.

The strangest thing was that some of those kids on that bus actually pitied me. "How can you stand living so far out from town?" they'd asked me. "It must take forever to get to the movies or go shopping."

I tried to explain to them that living on a ranch was the most wonderful thing in the world. Every day brought something new and exciting: baby calves in spring, champion ribbons at the summer horse show, the wonderful warm smell of my mother's baking when we came in cold and tired after taking feed to the stock in winter, and the good feeling of knowing both my parents were at home when I needed them. But the town kids didn't seem to understand, and I usually ended up by losing my temper and telling them they were dumb!

A sudden gust of wind hit me just then. It was so cold that it almost took my breath away. I shielded my eyes from the sun and stared out toward the mountains to the west.

The only clouds that drifted across the sky were harmless-looking white puffballs. So why could I smell snow?

"There can't be a storm yet," I pleaded. "At least not until after tomorrow!" The next day I would turn sixteen—old enough to drive, old enough to work, almost an adult. And I was going to have my first real, boy-girl party. I had wanted one the year before, but I didn't have a boy of my own to bring. This year I did—Ted—although I still found myself pinching my arm in disbelief.

Ted Brockman was one of the most popular guys in the school. Everyone looked up to him and everyone laughed a lot when he was around. I had gazed at him adoringly since freshman year and had never dreamed that he would ever notice me. After all, I wasn't a cheerleader. I wasn't an athlete—Ted played basketball and football. I wasn't in student government. I wasn't involved in any of the things he did so well. I certainly wasn't a beauty like his last girlfriend, a blonde who looked as if she'd stepped out of a hair spray commercial! I was tall and skinny, like a model, but my dark, uncontrollable hair was a beautician's nightmare.

I had Charlie to thank for meeting Ted. One afternoon, just a month before, he had escaped from the little field between the elementary school and the high school where I was allowed to keep him during the school day. I ran around in a panic. Everyone else had already gone home on the bus, and I didn't really know where to start looking. I had a horrible feeling that Charlie had decided to go home without me, and that I was in for a long walk.

Frantically, I dashed around the side of the old brick high school. There, like a vision, was Ted Brockman, leading Charlie by the reins.

"Is this horse yours?" Ted asked, taking one look at my face. I nodded. "You'd better tell him he can't be on the football team. We already have enough players, and besides our helmets won't fit him."

I started to giggle—from embarrassment mixed with relief. "I'm sorry," I managed to say. "I didn't know he liked to play."

Ted grinned. "You should have seen him. When we went to line up, he walked over and breathed down our necks."

"He always was a weird horse," I said, adding gratefully, "but you don't know how glad I am you found him. I thought I was in for a ten-mile walk home."

"You ride him to school?" Ted asked, surprised.

"Sure," I said. "He needs exercise and I hate the bus."

"Brave girl," he said, looking at me as if for the first time. "My name's Ted, by the way, what's yours?"

"It's Eden," I stammered, not wanting to

admit that I had known his name for two whole years.

"Like the Garden of?" Ted asked. "Pretty name. It suits you."

"Just don't forget and call me Eve," I said, surprised to hear myself say the words. "You wouldn't believe how many people have done that."

Ted laughed. It was a wonderful laugh, loud and musical and as real as the Wyoming Rockies. "I won't. Hey, I've got to get back to practice, but give me your phone number, Eden."

I scribbled it down for him on the back of an old math paper, then watched as he ran off with long, easy strides. That night he called me, and we went out together the following Saturday. Even my old-fashioned parents had to admit that he was somebody special.

I gave a long sigh of happiness as I turned Charlie to start to move down the hill and through the cornfields, urging him into a lope. *Tomorrow*, I thought, *I'll be dancing with Ted at my party.* All the girls would look at me with envy because he was so cute and so nice and so popular. *I've waited sixteen whole years for this,* I thought, *and it's been worth every minute of it.*

I wondered what Ted had bought me for my birthday. I hoped it was something pretty and romantic, like a piece of jewelry with our names engraved on it. Maybe he'd even give me his class ring! I couldn't wait to find out. I already knew what my parents had gotten me, even though they thought it'd be a surprise. They had bought me a new saddle for my jumping competitions. They knew I wanted one badly. For a whole year I had been dropping hints that I could turn Charlie into a first-class jumper if I had the proper equipment. After all, we had won everything in our class at the last show in Livingston.

I hadn't come right out and asked for the saddle because I knew things hadn't been going too well the past year. Cattle prices hadn't been good, and we'd lost a lot of stock to floods in the spring. But one of the things my dad was really enthusiastic about was my riding. He would come to all my shows, holding my ribbons so they would flutter in everyone's face, looking as proud as could be. He'd even watch me practice, leaning against the fence, not saying a word but watching our every move. And that evening at supper he'd say casually, "I got the feeling you were throwing your weight a bit far forward when you tried that trellis. Was I right?" He always was.

"How about that, Charlie?" I said out loud. "Tomorrow you and I get down to serious work together. No more bucking me off because you don't want to jump. I'm going to turn you into a champion. We'll go to all the big shows in Nebraska and Colorado. Ted can drive the horse trailer for us. Everything will be just perfect!"

As I talked, one cloud, darker than the others, moved across the sun for a second. I shivered, although we were lower down now and the wind wasn't blowing so hard.

"Come on, Charlie," I said. "Let's hurry on home." Charlie picked up my tension, and we flew down the trail. The school bus was just coming around the bend toward us, and for a while we moved parallel to each other. Some of the little kids leaned out of the windows and yelled things at me that I couldn't quite hear. Then the trail swung away again, across our own land and the stubble of last summer's hay crop.

I could see the house ahead, nestled behind its protective screen of trees. I paused for a moment, looking down at it fondly. It always seemed just perfect to me, the way it fit into the little hollow, with smoke curling up from the big brick chimney and the last of my mother's prize chrysanthemums blooming inside the white picket fence. As the trees swayed in the breeze a light caught my eyes. Something was flashing outside the house. I thought for a moment it was the sun reflecting off one of the windows. But as I got closer I could see it was the fire chief's car, its light still revolving.

Chapter Two

Hurriedly I slid from Charlie's back, hitching his reins to the fence rather than unsaddling him and putting him away as I usually did.

"Where's the fire?" I yelled, bursting into our big combination kitchen and family room. Birthday decorations hung from the walls and ceiling—I had already begun to get ready for the party. But the room was empty. Total silence. Nobody there.

At least I couldn't smell smoke. When you live out where we do, where summer winds can easily whip up prairie fires, your nose becomes very sensitive to the least whiff of smoke. But the only smell in the air was the pleasant aroma of warm baked goods, ready for my birthday party. My mother was the old-fashioned sort of housewife who believed a party was not a party without ten different kinds of pies and cakes, even though I kept telling her we'd be just as satisfied with barbequed chicken and potato chips.

Then I relaxed, walked across the room, and picked out an apple from the wooden bowl on the counter as I passed. False alarm. Mr. Heinrichs, the fire chief, one of my dad's old friends, had obviously just forgotten to turn off his light.

"Anyone home?" I yelled, walking through from the kitchen to the passageway beyond.

Without noticing me Mom scurried out of her bedroom at the end of the hall. One glance at her face, deathly white and suddenly old looking, and I knew something was very wrong.

"What is it, Mom?" I asked, feeling my stomach doing a horrible lurch.

"It's your daddy, Eden," she said, trying to keep her voice from shaking. "He's been taken bad. Jim Heinrichs has sent for the ambulance. It should be here any minute."

I moved toward their door, but my mother grabbed my arm. "No, don't go in now," she said. But I pulled myself free. I was sure he would want to see me—I might even make him feel better.

Jim Heinrichs looked up as I came in. He was sitting on the bed, taking Dad's pulse. His eyes were closed and his face was a horrible gray color. There were beads of sweat on his upper lip; damp hair lay like wet string across his forehead. I guess I must have given a little sob at the sight of him because he opened his eyelids. His lips twitched with the ghost of a smile.

"Is that you, Eden?" he whispered.

"Sure, Dad," I said, kneeling down beside him. "What happened to you?"

"Just had a bit of a bad turn," he said. "Guess I strained myself trying to lift those darned feed sacks. I'll be fine. Just need to rest awhile." He closed his eyes again as if talking had made him very tired.

"That's right, Dad, you take a good rest," I said, bending over him, "because you have to be well for my birthday tomorrow, remember? I can't have a party without my old dad there."

He nodded but didn't answer. For a long while I stared at him, feeling helpless and scared and angry.

My mother came up behind me and put her hand on my shoulder. "Leave your daddy in peace now, Eden," she whispered. "There's nothing you can do. There's nothing any of us can do until the ambulance gets here." I allowed her to lead me from the room.

"What's the matter with him?" I whispered as soon as we were out in the hall. "Is it pneumonia or something? He seems like he's running a fever with all that sweat."

She looked at me without blinking. "He's had a heart attack. Collapsed on the barn floor. Luckily Jim was able to get his heart going again, but he's worried your dad might have another attack before the ambulance gets here."

"A heart attack?" I blurted out, much louder than I intended. "Does that mean he's going to die?"

Again my mother put her finger to her lips. "If they can get him to the hospital in time, he's got a good chance," she said. "All we can do right now is hope."

"No!" I said, shaking my head in disbelief. "I don't want Daddy to die. They can't let him die. We've got to do something!"

"I don't want him to die, either, honey," Mom said softly and went back to her position by the bedroom door.

I wandered back through the family room, stopping to pick up a paper streamer from the floor. Happy Birthday was printed in pink all along it. I threw it down onto the sofa and bit my lip. I was not going to cry.

I went out through the front door, un-hitched Charlie, who was not in the best of tempers after being left tied up with his saddle on, and led him to his stall. I stood there, removing his saddle and bridle, hanging them up, brushing him down, giving him feed as if I were a robot. All the time I stared straight ahead of me, not allowing myself to think.

"Dad will be fine," I said to Charlie. "He's strong. Nothing gets the better of Dad!" And I went through all the memories I had stored away in my mind— Dad swinging half-grown calves onto the truck, picking me up and carrying me on his shoulders at the Fourth of July parade, and moving in the sofa he had had reupholstered for Mom's birthday. I couldn't remember his ever being sick enough to spend a day in bed. He was going to get over this right away, I was sure.

I kept repeating that over and over to myself as I watched the ambulance arrive. Two men jumped out with a stretcher, grabbed some intravenous equipment, and hurried into the house. A few minutes later they reappeared with Dad on the stretcher, and then they gently loaded the stretcher into the back of the ambulance.

Mom and I rode behind the ambulance to the hospital. "He's going to be fine," I muttered as a chant as the ambulance siren wailed ahead of us. I chanted on as we followed white-coated figures down long frightening hallways that smelled of disinfectant and pine cleaner, past open doors where frightening things hung from ceilings, past closed doors that said Danger, Radioactive Materials—Do Not Enter. I tried to keep on chanting it as we sat together, my mother and I, clutching hands on a black vinyl sofa in a small, white-tiled waiting room.

The hours passed as if in a dream. We sat without talking, pretending to read *American Sportsman* and *Golf Digest,* not wanting to ask each other what could be taking so long. Feet clattered past us, always in a hurry, and sometimes a distant voice yelled urgently. Each time we wondered if the voice was calling for extra help for my dad.

It was way past dinnertime when a large, bald, cheerful-looking doctor came to find us. He was the cardiologist, and he told us that Dad had a blood clot blocking an artery, which was stopping blood from getting to his heart. "We're going to operate to remove it. I'll check in with you to let you know how things are going," he announced.

I wanted to jump up, shake him, and shout, "It's my dad you're talking about!" Mom might have been feeling the same as me, but she didn't show it. She was very good at not showing her feelings. I heard her thanking the doctor for all his trouble.

I don't really remember more facts from that night, because I was so scared. But some impressions have stayed in my mind—the cold of the vinyl and the way it stuck to me when I leaned against it; the stale taste of the coffee in the cafeteria; the advertisements for long underwear in the outdoorsmen magazines. I also remember wishing I had brought my homework. Later a nurse invited us down to the TV lounge, but neither of us wanted to leave.

Then the surgeon came in to tell us that the clot had been removed successfully. I remember slumping back in relief, then looking at Mom in wordless joy. We smiled at each other. Then my eyes fell on the wall clock. It said two minutes past midnight.

"Hey, it's my birthday!" I said, feeling totally surprised. It felt as if I had moved to another planet where there were no such things as birthdays.

"Happy birthday," the doctor said. "Although it's not exactly the greatest way to celebrate, is it?"

"It's your birthday!" Mom said, also coming back out of a trance. "Oh, Eden, what are we going to do about the party and all those pies sitting on the counter?"

"It's OK, Mom," I said. "I'll just call everyone and postpone it. We can make room in the freezer for the pies, then we can have a celebration when Dad gets out of the hospital."

"Yes, that would be nice," Mom muttered, still half in a daze. "Your dad wouldn't want you to miss out on your party."

"Why don't you go home and get some rest?" the doctor asked kindly. "There's not much you can do here. He won't be out of the anesthetic for a while."

"I think I'll stay," my mother said, "just in case he wakes up."

"I'll stay, too," I said.

"Maybe you should go home and get some sleep," my mother suggested.

I shook my head. "I wouldn't want to let myself into an empty house. Anyway, I'd never sleep."

So we stayed, half dozing on the cold vinyl,

14

then waking with stiff necks. I'd finally drifted into an uneasy dream when a nurse came in with the news that Dad was awake and Mom could go in to him. I waited alone for what seemed like hours, too tense to drift off to sleep, until Mom came out again. "He seems to be OK," she said hesitantly. "He was asking for you. Maybe you'd like to pop in to see him."

I crossed the hall, and the nurse pushed open a heavy door for me. I stood very still in the doorway, feeling my heart beating very fast, looking from my father's still, gray face to the little green blip on the screen beside him that danced up and down. I began to feel very scared. Horrible thoughts started to fly through my head like maybe he was really dead and it was just all those electric things keeping him alive.

I crept closer and stood beside him. "Daddy?" I whispered. I saw his eyelids flutter before they opened and my dad's warm eyes focused on me.

"Eden!" he said, in a voice slightly louder than a whisper. "How's my girl?"

"I'm fine, Daddy. How are you?"

"Not too bad. Not too bad," he muttered. "Feeling a bit woozy still. Where's your mother?"

"They'd only let us in one at a time," I said. "She's back in the waiting room."

"Oh," he said. "You'd better take her home for dinner soon."

"Daddy, it's four o'clock in the morning," I said, smiling at him.

"Have I been here that long?" he asked. "I'd no idea. Have you been hanging around all this time?"

I nodded.

He smiled weakly. "You're a good girl, Eden," he said. "Take care of your ma for me."

"Don't talk like you're going to leave us, because you're not," I said, almost too brightly. "The doctor said you're going to be fine. You'll be back home with us before you know it."

He nodded, but didn't speak. Then he sighed. "And then there's those calves," he said. "Make sure José puts them away at night. Weather's getting cold now."

"Don't worry, Dad," I said. "We'll take care of everything. You just get yourself well." I bent down and gave him a kiss. His cheek felt cold.

He nodded. "Feeling a bit sleepy," he muttered. "Think I'll get some rest. You're a good girl, Eden. Take your ma home and get some rest yourself. No sense in hanging around here watching me sleep."

"OK, Dad," I said. "We'll be back when you wake up again."

But he didn't answer. He was already asleep, his eyes shut and his face peaceful. I tiptoed from the room.

Chapter Three

No matter what Dad had said, my mother refused to go home. She did promise to get herself some breakfast in the cafeteria, though, after she drove me home to get some sleep. I agreed to go, knowing that was what she wanted.

The house felt very strange as I let myself in—cold and empty, as if nobody had lived there for a long while.

I wandered around, trying to get my head back in working order, wondering what things needed to be done before I could go to bed. The phone calls to cancel my party could wait until later—after all, not many of my friends got up at seven-thirty on a Saturday morning. I plugged in the coffee pot and put the pies in the freezer. Then I shoved a couple of

17

frozen waffles into the toaster, although I didn't really feel like eating anything.

I felt scared and lonely, and I wanted someone to talk to. I thought about phoning Ted, but I didn't. I could hardly ask him to come over that early just to keep me company. I looked at the telephone several times, then took my waffles out and poured syrup over them, chewing them mechanically.

After I'd eaten about half a waffle, I couldn't swallow any more, so I went out to find José. As I had suspected, he had everything under control, and, through that uncanny grapevine that exists among ranch hands, he knew all about my father.

"Please tell him that I hope he gets well quickly," he said in his heavy accent. "He's a good boss, Mr. Harrison."

Then I checked on Charlie and went back into the house. "Just a few minutes' rest," I muttered to myself. "Then I can face the day."

I lay down on the sofa and covered myself with an old afghan Grandma had crocheted. Next thing I knew bells were ringing wildly. I leaped up, my heart pounding. For some reason I thought the bell was another ambulance, but it was only the telephone. I snatched it up.

" 'Happy birthday to you, happy birthday to you, happy birthday, dear Eden, happy birthday to you,' " sang a deep voice, slightly out of tune. I listened to it all the way through, not knowing whether to laugh or cry.

"Aren't you going to say something?" Ted demanded. "Or has my wonderful singing left you speechless?"

"Sorry, Ted," I mumbled. "You just woke me. It was terrific singing."

"Just woke you?" he asked. "It's past eleven. I thought you country folk were up with the birds and bees."

"I didn't get any sleep last night."

"Hey, what's this?" he demanded suspiciously. "You aren't allowed to party without me around."

"Some party," I said. "I was at the hospital all night. My dad had a heart attack, Ted."

There was a pause on the other end of the line. "Gee, I'm sorry," he muttered. "Me and my big mouth. Is he OK?"

"I hope so," I said. "They had to operate to remove a blood clot in an artery. I saw him this morning and he didn't look too wonderful, but then I don't suppose I'd look too great after a heart attack and surgery. The doctor says he'll make it."

"Hey, he's a strong guy, your dad," Ted said encouragingly. "I bet he'll be up and around in no time." There was another pause. "Boy, what a tough birthday for you," he said.

"It's OK," I said, trying to sound bright again. "When you get to my age, who wants birthdays?"

"You'll have to cancel your party, won't you?"

"Yeah. I'd better start calling everyone," I said.

"You want me to do it for you?" he asked.

"Would you mind?"

"It's the least I can do," he said.

"Oh, Ted, that'd be great." I sighed, relieved. "I was dreading doing it."

"But we can still celebrate together," he said. "I want to give you my present."

"I'd really like that, Ted," I said. "It's so strange and empty over here."

"I'll make the calls, then come right over," he said.

He was as good as his word. Barely an hour later his battered red truck came bouncing down the driveway and pulled to a stop outside the house. I ran out to meet him.

"Gee, you look terrible," he said as he took me into his arms.

"Thanks a million," I said. "You sure know how to flatter a girl."

He looked at me through sheepish eyes. "I mean you look very nice for a worried daughter who was up all night. Have you eaten yet? I've got some hamburgers and shakes in the truck."

"Oh, Ted," I said, resting my head against his big, strong shoulder and feeling myself relax for the first time since the day before. "I'm so glad you're here. It's been a nightmare."

"I bet it has," he said, putting his big arm around me and steering me toward the house. "But don't worry, I'm here now and everything's going to be just fine."

Ted treated me like a princess, laying the table with cloth napkins and putting the hamburgers daintily on plates. I couldn't keep from laughing.

"You're a crazy guy," I said between mouthfuls of hamburger. "But I'm so glad you're around!"

"Oh, before I forget," he said, looking a bit embarrassed as he fished into his pocket, "I've got this for you."

I opened the package and inside was a chain made of foil blobs. I looked at it suspiciously. "What is it?" I asked.

Ted looked hurt. "Can't you tell?" he asked. "It's a Hershey's Kiss for every day we've been together."

"Oh," I said, trying to look pleased although it was hardly the present I'd been expecting. I counted thirty-two kisses. "You've blown it," I said. "Even counting today we've only been together thirty-one days."

He grinned. "Dumb of me," he said. "I wonder why I put an extra one in there?"

I felt the last one. The heavy blob wasn't made of candy at all, but of silver.

"Here's the chain to go with it," he said and helped me put the silver charm around my neck.

"This is wonderful," I said, feeling the tears scratching at the back of my eyes. "I'll never take it off." I turned to look at him. "You know I was feeling so down this morning. I felt that nothing would ever go right again. But this isn't such a bad birthday."

I would have said more, but Ted stopped me with a long, lingering kiss that was the best birthday present of all.

Chapter Four

During the next few days Mom spent every moment with Dad, and I spent every moment working feverishly to keep myself from worrying. Ted drove me in to visit Dad in the evenings, and although he was weak, he seemed to be getting better.

"What you need is some of Mom's special stew," I told him as I watched him pick at a tray of orange Jell-O and pale brown broth. "And plenty of dumplings floating around in it!"

He managed a weak smile. "That's what I need," he agreed.

"If you're not careful, I'll make you my brownies," I threatened. I was famous in my family for my lack of cooking skills.

Any other time he would have come back

with a wisecrack, but now he merely nodded and turned his head to the wall.

"It's bound to take awhile," Ted said as we drove home together. "You don't get over anything as major as a heart attack in a few days."

"I know," I said. But I just hated seeing him like that. He'd always been so proud of the work he could do and how he could still toss the bales of hay by himself.

Two weeks went by, and Dad continued to improve very slowly. I'd fallen asleep in front of an old movie one evening when Mom came back very late.

"Is that you, Mom?" I asked, startled.

She noticed me curled up on the sofa. "Eden, what on earth are you doing there?" she asked. "It's past midnight."

"I was trying to wait up for you," I said. "But I guess I fell asleep."

"You shouldn't have done that, honey," she said, sitting down beside me. After a long pause she added, "I saw the specialist again." She sank back into the sofa and gave a big sigh.

"How's Dad coming along?" I asked. "Is the specialist pleased?"

She sighed again. "We all had a long talk tonight," she said. "We had to do some planning about the future."

"The future?" I asked. "Dad is going to be OK, isn't he?"

She looked at me with tired, kind eyes. "It's not going to be easy, Eden," she said. "Dad's heart has been permanently damaged. He'll never be able to do hard physical work again. No more digging or lifting or anything like that. He'll only stay alive if he takes things easy."

"Oh," I said. "I bet Dad didn't like that. He won't like to sit back and watch other people doing hard work on the ranch. José can help out pretty well, but he just doesn't have the experience with cattle yet—"

"Eden," my mother cut in. I stopped talking. There was silence, except for the old movie still crackling on the TV. "Eden," my mother said again, "we'll have to sell the ranch."

"Sell the ranch!" I exploded. "We can't! Where would we go?"

"I'm afraid we have to, honey," my mother said.

"But why? We could find someone to run it, I know we could."

My mother shook her head. "It wouldn't work, honey," she said. "Even if we could find the right man, we couldn't afford to pay him. You know we haven't been doing very well these past years. Your daddy's going to need continual medical care, and besides, I don't want him tempted to start throwing up a few bales of hay when the men are not doing it to his liking. You know what he's like. He'd never sit back and watch someone else round up his cattle."

"But w-where would we go?" I stammered. "What would we do? What would happen to the ranch and the cattle?"

She sighed again. "We decided the best thing—the only thing—to do is sell everything, stock and all, and move to the city."

"The city!" I cried. "You mean Cheyenne?"

"No, Denver," my mother said.

"Denver! But that's miles away!" I could hardly make the words come out. My mind pictured lots of imposing big city skyscrapers, cars, and strange people. I could feel my knees trembling as if I were very cold. "But we don't belong in a city," I said. "We'd all hate it!"

"Your dad needs to be close to a good medical center," my mother said. "And we need to find work. When he's stronger, he'd like to look for a small business—maybe buy a hardware store."

"A hardware store!" I blurted out before I could stop myself. "But if we sell the ranch, won't we have enough money to live on? You could invest it at the bank, and Dad wouldn't have to work at all."

"Eden," my mother said, "we've kept a lot of things from you because your dad didn't want you to worry. But the truth is, we're very heavily in debt. If we sell the ranch, the bank gets most of it. We'll have enough to get ourselves a small place to live, but nothing more."

I stared at the TV set, feeling like a fairy

tale princess who was turned into a goose
girl with one swoop of a magic wand. I tried
to run it through my head in logical se-
quence—no more ranch, no more Wheatland
High School, no more friends I had grown up
with since kindergarten. "Charlie?" I asked.
"What will happen to Charlie?"

Mom reached over and took my hand. "Look,
Eden. You're strong like your daddy. I want
you to be very brave right now, because both
your daddy and I are going to need your help.
Quite frankly I don't know how I'm going to
make it, either. Cities scare me—you know
that—and your daddy has always taken care
of everything. But I want him to have the
best medical care. I want to keep him alive,
Eden, and I know you do, too."

I nodded. I didn't trust my voice to say
anything.

She got to her feet. "Well, let's go to sleep.
Things always look brighter in the morning.
Maybe Mary Alice has room in her field for
Charlie. I understand they want a pony for
Jason."

She patted my shoulder and walked ahead
of me to her room. I tried to imagine Charlie
with fat little Jason O'Brien, my friend's youn-
ger brother, on his back. Charlie had seemed
like such a giant horse when I was seven years
old and Dad had first brought him home. I
remembered how we learned to jump together
and how he'd soared over that big gate at the
last horse show. I'd been sitting all wrong on

his back, but he just tucked his legs in and got over it without any help from me. We could have made a great team, Charlie and I. I'd had such great dreams for the two of us. Now none of it was going to happen. Just a few seconds when my dad's heart had stopped beating had changed my whole life.

I think I spent so much time thinking about Charlie because it helped block out my most unsettling thought—I would be leaving Ted, too. It was so unfair. We'd grown even closer since Dad's illness; Ted spent practically every free minute he had with me. Why did I have to lose him now when I needed him the most?

"Hey, Denver isn't half bad," he said when I broke the news to him the next morning. "I wouldn't mind moving to Denver. Much better than a dead dump like this."

"You sound as if you're anxious to get rid of me!" I exclaimed.

He took my face in his hands. "Of course I'm not, you dummy," he said, smiling down at me. "But it's only a hundred miles, and that's not so far away. We'll be zooming up and down the interstate to see each other all the time."

"I only know how to drive a tractor," I said. "Can you see me zooming up the highway in a tractor?"

Ted laughed. "Maybe you'll get yourself a real city-girl car, and you'll come back and look down on us poor country folk!"

"I'd never do that," I said, horrified at the suggestion. "I won't ever be a city girl—however long we live there."

I tried to think calmly about moving to the city those next few weeks while real estate people tramped around our place and peered into my closets. Half the time I couldn't believe it was really happening. I'd look at Charlie, look at the hills already dusted with snow, and try to imagine a window that opened onto streets and tall buildings. Would I ever belong there? Would I ever find friends and fun in a distant city?

"I think you're being terrific about all this," my best friend, Jodi, said one afternoon as we did our homework together. "I know I'd have cried and made a fuss if we had to leave and move to the city, but you're being so brave!"

I managed a smile. "If you only knew how I feel inside," I said. "But my mother's one step away from collapsing, so one of us has to keep going, and I guess that's me."

Jodi reached out and rested her hand on my shoulder. "Poor Eden," she said. "Look, if there's anything I can do . . ."

"Not unless you happen to have a few hundred thousand dollars to buy a ranch," I said with a grin. "I hate having those real estate people nosing through our house."

It was snowing when Mom and Jim Heinrichs brought Dad into the house one mid-

November afternoon. It was the first real snow of the year.

"Here's Santa Claus a month early!" Dad laughed as he caught sight of his face in the mirror. "Look at me, all white and covered with snow. I never saw myself with a white face before. I need to get back on a horse again!"

"Jake Harrison, you're not getting back on any horse again," my mother said fiercely. "You know what you promised the doctor, and I'm going to make sure you keep that promise. None of this sneaking out to help with the calves!"

I looked at her, amazed. My mother was always the quiet one. To hear her barking an order was something totally new to me. Equally new was watching Dad accept the order. "OK, OK," he said, sinking into his favorite chair. "I've got to take things easy. You don't have to tell me."

As I watched him sink into that chair it hit me with a jolt that this was how things were going to be from then on. Deep down I think I had secretly believed that he would make a miraculous recovery the moment he came home. He'd be back to his old, energetic self, and those dumb doctors would have to admit they were wrong. Now I knew that I was the one who was wrong: I had expected him to be a terrible patient, refusing to sit down and constantly trying to sneak outside, but instead he sat quietly and did what my mother told him. He hardly showed any interest in anything around him.

He was only mildly interested in the woman who came to look at our house that afternoon. But my mother was horrified. "Imagine, Jake," she whispered. "She wanted to know where she could put her microwave and her trash compactor, and she thought she could put a sauna in a closet. What exactly is a sauna, Eden?"

"It's a little room. You get it really hot and then you sit there and sweat," I said.

Both my parents managed to laugh at this. "I can tell them plenty of ways to work up a sweat without having to sit in a little room," Dad said, sounding for a moment like his old self.

"Why would someone like that want our house?" I asked, puzzled.

My mother sniffed disapprovingly. "Her husband was born on a ranch like this, and he's always wanted a place to relax on weekends."

I thought of my father getting up at five every day of his life, going out in the middle of a blizzard because some cattle were lost, and delivering calves in the middle of the night. And these people wanted to come here to relax! It was as if everything Dad had worked for was being betrayed.

"They'll never buy it, will they?" I asked hopefully.

But two days later, when I came home from

school, there was a signed sales agreement on our kitchen table.

"They offered a real fair price, Eden," my mother said, looking at the hurt I couldn't hide in my face. "And they want to keep the stock. Makes it simpler all around!"

"I'd better start packing," I said, turning away and walking to my room.

"There's no need to rush, honey," Mom said, putting her head around the door. "We have a few weeks." But I began shoving things into boxes as if hard work would drive away the volcano that was ready to explode inside my head. I knew I had no right to feel angry at my parents—after all, they didn't want to leave their home any more than I did. But, however hard I tried, the anger would not go away. I put on a bright face and did my chores, and nobody knew that inside I was about to explode.

I kept up my bright face while the movers came right before Christmas vacation and carried out our furniture. I even kept it when Dad and I were going through the toolshed and we sat down to sort out the tools we'd take to our new home and found the birthday saddle everyone had forgotten.

"Oh," he said, as I pulled off the sacking and looked down at the new, shiny saddle. "Oh, Eden, honey, I'm so sorry. Everything's spoiled for you."

"It's OK," I said, swallowing hard. "Charlie would have made a terrible fuss. You know how he hated anything new, and he never did like jumping anyway." I babbled on, trying to sound as if I didn't care.

I even managed to say goodbye to Ted without crying. He came over after the moving truck had trundled off toward Denver.

"I'm not the world's best writer," he said, wrapping me in his arms. "But I'll call. And I'll be down to see you as often as I can."

I nodded because I didn't dare use my voice.

"And, Eden," he said. "Look, you'll be going to a new school, meeting new friends. I really like you and I really like having you as my special girl, but if you find someone you like down there, I'll understand." I nodded mutely, too shocked to speak. Was this how it was going to end between us?

He kissed me, then released me and quickly turned away. Then suddenly he turned back.

"I didn't mean that," he said. "If even one of those city boys comes anywhere near you, I'll break every bone in his body!"

"Oh, Ted," I said, half laughing and crying at the same time. "I'm going to miss you so much."

I kept back the tears until he had gone, waving until the red truck was just a speck bouncing along the fields of stubble. Then I saddled up Charlie and rode him over to the O'Briens'. That day even Charlie didn't want to go fast. As if he sensed something was wrong, he plodded along with his head down.

Mary Alice and her four brothers and sisters all crowded around him, telling him how pretty he was. They brought out sugar lumps and pieces of carrot, and he took them all graciously, like visiting royalty. I thought I would just sneak away while he was busy eating. I would keep on being brave, I had decided. Everyone would say how wonderful and brave I'd been through everything. But this time I couldn't stop the tears.

I didn't want all those little kids to see me crying. I turned and hurried out of the field, hoping that Charlie wouldn't notice. But when I was already down the road and I turned back for one last look, he was standing there by the fence, staring after me, watching me go.

Chapter Five

My first few days in Denver were really scary. The buildings were so tall, the people doing their last-minute Christmas shopping were in so much of a hurry, and cars seemed to hoot at me every time I tried to step off a curb. All the other people seemed to know where they were going and to be totally at ease as they dodged in and out of the traffic— even little kids. My folks found the city equally terrifying, so I kept my own fears shut away and ran out to do errands for them instead.

Our new home was in the Steinhart Apartments, not far from the middle of town and just a stone's throw from a major medical center. It was a big, impersonal yellow-brick building with a canopy over the front door and faded red carpet in the hallway. I think it might have been elegant once, but now it was just tired and old. The whole building smelled of other people's stale cooking and pine cleaners. I felt like an intruder every time I walked down the dark hallway staring at the blank doors, wondering if I'd ever make friends with the people who lived behind them.

When I looked out my window on the fourth floor, all I could see were more buildings stretching into the distance. I think it would have made settling in a bit easier if I could have seen hills. I had no idea Denver would be so flat. My father said you could see the Rockies out toward the west, but not from our apartment.

On our second day I was making my way down the dark hall after running out for a carton of milk, peering at the numbers because all the doors looked the same, when a girl coming out of an open door nearly collided with me.

She was tiny, with a round face and black hair cut in a short, bouncy bob. Slowly her surprised expression turned into a smile. "Gee, you scared the daylights out of me," she said. "You must be one of the new folks who moved in down the hall."

"That's right," I said, feeling in no mood for a chat right then.

"I'm Trisha," she said. "What's your name?"

"Eden," I said, already looking down the hall to our door.

"Welcome to Denver, Eden," she went on brightly. "How do you like your apartment?"

"It's OK, if you like living in a dark cereal box, I suppose," I said. "But it doesn't matter because we won't be staying long."

I saw her face fall as I turned away. She had tried to be friendly and I snubbed her. Too late I realized that her apartment must be pretty much like ours. By saying terrible things about our apartment I had insulted hers, too. I looked back, but her door was already closed again.

That afternoon when I saw Trisha again in the hall I ran to catch up with her. "Look, I'm sorry about this morning," I said. "I really didn't mean to be rude like that."

"It's OK," she said, nodding as if she understood. "My mom told me that your dad's just had a bad heart attack. People don't act like themselves when they're worried. It must have been awful for you."

I nodded. "Pretty bad," I said. "Having to give up our ranch in Wyoming and move here was the worst thing that ever happened to me."

"Oh, but think of all the good things about living in Denver," Trisha said. "You get the latest movies and concerts, and the latest fashions are in the stores. Will you be going to Evans High?"

"Yes," I said. "I'll be starting right after vacation. My parents have enough to worry about right now." I heard my voice quiver as

I said this, and I swallowed hard so that I didn't start crying again.

Trisha looked at me with dark, understanding eyes, and I wished I knew her better so that I could share my worries with someone. But I could hardly blurt out my troubles to someone I'd just met. Instead I took a deep breath and managed to smile. "I guess it'll take awhile to get used to being here," I said.

"You have to give it time," she said. "My mom had an operation last year, and it took a long time before she was back to normal again. Things will be better when you're in school and you've got some friends. I know you'll like Evans. I'm a senior and I know most people, so I can help you settle in."

"Thanks," I said. "I'm going to need all the help I can get."

"I'd better be going," Trisha said, looking at her watch, "or I'll be late for work."

"Where do you work?" I asked.

"I help in a day care center," she said. "I wouldn't recommend it unless you love screaming kids. See ya!"

Christmas approached almost without our noticing it. Neither of my parents had much enthusiasm for it this year. My father was usually the bright one when it came to exciting Christmas ideas and surprises, but he wasn't allowed to do any shopping. My mother was famous for her nonstop Christmas baking, but this year she had no time to bake anything.

One of the first things she had done after we unpacked our things was to get a job. It was clear that we needed money until my father was strong enough to get started in business, but I was amazed at the way she calmly announced that she was going to be working in the gift wrap department of the big store around the corner. Was this the same mother who fussed and hesitated about driving into town at home, who was a nervous wreck before PTA meetings, and who hated crowds? I realized at that moment how very much Dad meant to her. She was willing to go into a new, strange, and frightening world because somebody had to make money in our family.

She came home horrified after her first day. "You should see them, Jake," she told my father. "All that money just to put some fancy paper around a couple of boxes! And impatient! Everyone's in a big rush, all yelling at me to get a move on and they haven't got all day to stand there!"

I heard this from the kitchen where I was making her a cup of coffee. It was easy to hear everything because the apartment walls were paper thin and the rooms were very small. She sounded so tired and upset. I began to feel very guilty. Maybe I should have insisted that I get a job, too. But Mom wanted me to stay home to help Dad. *After Christmas,* I thought, *when I've settled in at school and feel like I belong a bit more, then I must get a job.*

We awoke to a white Christmas. We sat around, just the three of us, sipping coffee and opening presents, all pretending that it was another time and another place. I hadn't known what to get for either of my parents. Dad had never done anything except work on the ranch and had never worn anything except ranch clothes before. After much thought, I got him one of those little personal stereos so that he could listen to music when he woke up in the middle of the night, something he did quite often these days. I got my mother a pretty lilac blouse, because all of her clothes were ranch clothes, too, and those impatient city women needed to see that gift wrappers could dress nicely. I spent the last of my savings account on their gifts, but it was worth it to see their surprised and pleased faces.

Then I opened my parents' present to me. It was in a big box, gift wrapped at my mother's store. Inside I found a white leather jacket, black cords, a striped shirt, a red fuzzy sweater, and a slim gray skirt. I stood looking at them with my mouth open.

"Mom," I said, shaking my head in disbelief. "You shouldn't have! These must have cost a fortune!"

"Don't you like them?" my mother asked defensively.

"Of course! I love them," I said.

"Well, you kept saying that you wouldn't have the right clothes to wear to a city school," she said. "And I know how important clothes are to girls your age. So I asked Mrs. Klemperer who works with me and has a daughter about your age, and she helped me select the sort of clothes the kids wear around here."

I picked them up one at a time, the soft leather jacket, smelling a little like my saddle, the silky blouse, the fuzzy sweater. "And they all go together, too," I said, holding the sweater up against me. "But you still shouldn't have spent this much."

"Don't worry about that, Eden," my father said. "Your mom gets a discount at the store. Besides, we never gave you a proper birthday present, remember?"

After that I tried extra hard to be bright and cheerful all day. I helped my mother with the turkey, I peeled the vegetables, and I put a Christmas carol record on the stereo. And we all pretended to be having the best Christmas of our lives.

Right after lunch the next day Ted called, which was the best surprise I could have had. We couldn't have much of a conversation because there was a noisy party going on at his house and bursts of wild laughter and music kept interrupting us, but it was wonderful to hear his voice.

"I've got the basketball team here," he said.

"We're celebrating beating the Wildcats. You know what that means, don't you?"

They were Wheatland's biggest rivals. Ted's bubbling enthusiasm contrasted sharply with the quiet of my afternoon. Dad was dozing in his chair, and Mom was at work. I couldn't think of anything upbeat to tell Ted about my future. For the first time in our relationship I was left speechless.

"I can't talk with all this noise going on," he yelled at last. "I'll have to come down on Sunday and tell you in person."

"Ted's coming down on Sunday!" I yelled, dancing excitedly to my father. At least there was one thing to look forward to again.

He arrived on Sunday in time for lunch. Mom had the weekend off and had made one of her famous stews with the remains of the turkey. Cornbread floated on top of it and a blueberry pie followed for dessert. It really hurt her to go out and buy canned fruit for the pie—she had always used her own bottled fruit before—but it was just as good as any pie she had baked.

I wish Ted's visit had been as satisfying. But after his kiss hello, which seemed too abrupt for me, the day went downhill.

Ted's six-foot-plus frame seemed to fill our tiny apartment, and his voice seemed somehow too loud. He must have felt a little ill at ease, too, because he perched on the edge of his chair and played with his napkin a lot. After lunch we went for a walk together. It was slippery underfoot and the city snow had turned to gray slush. He held my hand and gave me all the news from home, especially about the last basketball game.

"I probably won't be down again for a while," he said. "The games are going to keep me pretty busy till March, but I'll let you know how we're doing."

In a deserted park he stopped and kissed me, and his lips were warm against my cold ones. But even his kiss didn't make me feel less miserable. We had always talked so easily before, but this time there had been silences. If a barrier was growing up this quickly between us, what chance did our relationship have for the future?

Chapter Six

A week later I started at Evans High. The campus was unlike anything I'd ever seen. A huge lawn and a flight of white steps led up to an elegant, classically styled building with Greek columns. In fact, when I went with my mother to register, we drove right past it, thinking that it was the city hall or a library or something. Trisha called for me on that first morning of school and walked with me up the steps to the office. "I'll try to see you at lunchtime to find out how you're getting along," she said before she disappeared down the hallway.

I stood for a moment outside the office door, taking a deep breath and watching hundreds of unknown faces stream past me. I was very glad for the white leather jacket and the black cords. My old jeans and flannel shirts would definitely not fit in here.

Soon after I arrived I noticed one group of girls who looked as if they had stepped out of a fashion magazine. They all had perfect hair and painted fingernails and trendy clothes. They were talking and laughing together. As they passed me, a tall blonde in a white angora sweater decorated with pearls shook her head in disbelief and laughed heartily. Her shoulder-length curls swung from side to side and fell back into place as she said in a low, musical voice, "You're kidding. That didn't really happen, did it?"

I gazed after them wistfully. Back home I'd been part of a group like that, laughing and sharing secrets. Would I ever belong here? How would I ever get to know people in this big, strange school?

At the guidance office I was given a schedule and I walked behind a counselor to my first English class. I was horribly conscious of thirty pairs of eyes watching me as I entered the room.

"There's a spare place beside you, Miss McArtle, isn't there?" the teacher asked. I saw that my neighbor was none other than the pretty blonde. She moved her books from my desk and gave me a quick smile as I sat down.

The class was much harder than my English class at home, and I was exhausted from all my concentrating by the time the bell rang.

"First day here?" Renee McArtle asked as I gathered up my books.

"That's right," I said. "And from the level of that English class, I don't know how long I'm going to last."

She grinned. "I know what you mean. Mr. Hollis is tough. What do you have next?"

"Biology," I said, looking down at my schedule.

"That's down the stairs to the six hundred hall," she said. "Have you got Carter or Stevens?"

I consulted the schedule again. "Carter."

"She's nice. You won't have any problems with her," Renee said. She gathered up her books and walked out beside me. "I've got chorus now," she said. "But if you want to join us for lunch, we're always at the end of the cafeteria, by the windows."

"Thanks," I mumbled gratefully. I could scarcely believe my luck. It was almost as if a good fairy had heard my wish to join a group like that and waved a wand.

At lunch, however, I found that joining a new group was not so simple as it sounded.

"This is the new girl from my English class," Renee said to the group as I hovered behind their table. "Here, squeeze in next to Paula. Move over, fatso!"

Paula giggled and made room for me. She

was very thin and very beautiful. "Did you just move here?" she asked.

I nodded.

"Where from?" a sleek, dark-haired girl asked.

"Wyoming," I said.

"Wyoming!" the girl said. "Wow, welcome to civilization!" They all laughed.

"I never got your name," Renee interrupted. "I'm Renee, by the way and this is Paula, Kathy, Anita, Debbie, and Sue." She rattled them off so quickly I had no chance to see which name belonged to whom.

"I'm Eden," I said.

Renee looked impressed. "Nice name," she said. "And I like your outfit."

"Thanks," I mumbled, wondering what they were going to say when they found out it was practically my only outfit.

Renee then turned her attention to the others, leading a discussion about the ski trips they'd all taken over the holidays. "We rented a place at Breckenridge," she said. "The skiing wasn't as great as Aspen but the people were friendlier."

Paula chimed in, "I'll take Vail over all of them. I heard the ski club's going there in two weeks. I can't wait!" Then to my surprise, she turned to me. "Are you going to join us?"

I didn't know what to say. How could I tell these gorgeously dressed girls I didn't have the money for fancy ski trips? "Um, I don't know," I hedged.

"You ski, don't you?" Renee pressed.

"I've been to Jackson," I said. At least I didn't have to lie—though it was a stretch of the truth. I'd been on a ski slope exactly one time as part of a 4-H trip. Inwardly I winced, remembering how many times I fell.

"I love it there," Sue said. "So you'll come with us?"

I could feel the pressure of six sets of eyes staring at me. If I said the wrong thing they might not want me to go. But on the other hand I didn't see how I could fit into their way of life. "I'll let you know," I finally answered.

For the rest of the lunch I didn't say anything. I felt increasingly removed from these girls as they chatted about new movies and rock concerts and who was dating whom. They could have been talking about nuclear physics as far as I was concerned. It was all so alien and frightening.

Yet, to her credit, Renee sensed my uneasiness.

"I know how hard it must be to come to a new school as a junior," she went on. "You'll feel better once you meet the whole gang. There are some really cute boys at this school, too. We'll have to fix you up with one."

"I already have a perfectly good boyfriend at home," I said, before I could stop myself. Automatically I reached for the silver charm around my neck.

"Oh, really?" Renee said, eyeing the charm. Then she started talking to somebody else.

After lunch Paula walked to American history with me.

"Do you think you're going to like it here?" she asked as we walked upstairs.

"I've only been here a couple of hours," I said, "so I can't really judge yet."

She smiled. "Let me give you some advice. If you want to fit in here, don't get on Renee's bad side. She loves playing matchmaker around here."

I felt my cheeks turn pink. "I shouldn't have snapped at her. I just wanted to let her know that I didn't need to be fixed up with any boy."

"So you're still going steady with a boy back home?"

I nodded. "There's no way I could look at anyone else," I said.

Paula sighed. "It must be true love if you can stay together when you're so far apart. I wish I had a boy like that!"

I thought about Paula's remarks all through class. Did Ted really feel like that about me? We had hardly seen each other since I left. How long would I stay his special girl if we never got a chance to see each other? I had to find out about driver's ed. The sooner I learned to drive something other than a tractor, the better.

I saw Trisha briefly in the hall. "Surviving so far?" she asked.

"So far," I said. "I've met a nice girl called Renee McArtle who seems to have taken me under her wing."

Trisha looked impressed. "Well, if Renee likes you, you're in," she said. "You won't need my help, which is good because you should see this paper I have to research for English! Between homework and the day care center, I barely have time to breathe these days. I can't wait for college and a calm life again!"

Then she hurried off, like a miniature whirlwind. An image popped into my mind of a good fairy, appearing and disappearing every now and then with advice. *Nobody seems to have time for anything in this city,* I thought, still feeling confused by the way everyone rushed around.

"So how was school?" my parents asked later as we all sat down to dinner.

"OK, I guess."

"Did you meet any nice kids?"

"A group of girls invited me to have lunch with them."

"Oh, that's wonderful, Eden," my mother said. "I knew you'd fit in."

"I don't know about that," I said. "They all look like Brooke Shields."

My mother laughed. "Well, you look pretty nice, too, in that new outfit."

"School's going to be hard," I said. "You should see the homework I have tonight!"

"Oh, I almost forgot. I picked up the mail, and there's a letter for you from Jodi," my mother said, waving it at me. "I must say she's a very faithful writer."

"Much better than Ted," I muttered to myself.

After dinner I took it into my room and closed the door. Jodi's letter was full of news about the basketball team's success and about the big storm that had left some of the ranchers cut off for days. "The school bus couldn't even get through to us," Jodi wrote. "You can imagine how upset we were about it! Those new folks were out at your place for the weekend and got snowed in. I wonder if they still think ranching is so much fun now?"

As soon as I finished her letter I got out some paper to write back:

I started my new school today, and frankly it's like being at school on another planet. I was really excited when this fashionable-looking girl Renee invited me to eat lunch with her group, but there was no way I could join in their conversation.

I think maybe I'm at the wrong high school. All the girls dress like models. Everyone but me seems to be stinking rich—you should see the cars parked out front! I've got to get a job real soon, Jodi.

I think it will be a long time before my dad gets that hardware store. So far he's only left the apartment to go to his doctor. Sometimes I'm not sure all this rest and quiet is the best thing for him. He needs to fight. My mother is his worst enemy. She keeps soothing him and treating him like a baby. And I feel like I'm ready to explode!

Dad was always a fighter, I thought as I folded up the letter and slipped it into an envelope. *But it's as if giving up the ranch has made him give up his will to live! He's just not trying anymore.* I wanted to shake him, do anything to make him snap back to being his old self.

Chapter Seven

By February I thought I'd be settled in Denver, but it didn't work out that way. I ate lunch with Renee and her friends every day, but I still felt strange with them because I wasn't included in their out-of-school activities. It didn't bother me all the time since I still had my hands full adjusting to the heavier, tougher schoolwork. But late at night when I allowed myself to feel the loneliness I tried to pretend didn't exist, I turned my thoughts to the one person I really cared about—Ted.

I still daydreamed about being with him, but I didn't know if he still thought about me. I hadn't seen him since that Sunday he came down. True to his word he hardly ever wrote, and the only time he had phoned was to tell me that Wheatland had beaten the Laramie Cougars and was now a cinch to win the conference championship. What that meant was that he wouldn't have time to drive to Denver.

"You do understand, don't you, Eden?" he asked during that phone call. "I'd really like to see you again, but I can't let the team down. Not now, when we're so close to the championship."

"Sure, I understand," I said, trying to keep my voice even. I kept thinking that what he really meant was that he wasn't missing me as much as I was missing him. That was logical, I told myself. His life was in full swing, while I was standing on the sidelines wondering which way to turn. The girls in Renee's group were nice to me, and I was glad to have someone to eat lunch with. But most of the time I was on my guard, like a spy, waiting to invent experiences I hadn't had.

What I needed most was someone to talk to. In the past I would have spilled everything to my parents, but I couldn't do that any more. Mom had a busy life of her own now, working for the department store. She'd been promoted from being a gift wrapper to a salesperson in fine china. She now came home every day talking about Noritake and Wedgwood. The department manager was pregnant, and my mother thought she might get her job when the manager left. All of this was totally bewildering to me. I had never dreamed that my mother would enjoy working in a store. She had always been rather shy and preferred to stay home in her own kitchen rather than get mixed up in volunteer programs. But now she was clearly enjoying every minute of her day at the store. She traded her old shapeless shirts and sweaters for new smart outfits. She had her hair cut in a sleek new style, and she started wearing makeup for the first time that I could remember.

"I'm still surviving," I wrote in my next letter to Jodi.

Dad is showing some signs of improvement—at least he's stopped watching soap operas all day—but he's still pretty depressed and tired. Mom seems to like her job and I'm really happy for her. The one bad thing is that she doesn't have any time anymore. You remember how she used to cook up a storm for every meal? Now we're lucky to get a hamburger—and most of the time I have to cook it. Actually I'm glad to be busy, because it stops me from thinking of home too much. Mom doesn't seem to miss it at all, and I can't talk to Dad about how lonely I feel because I'm supposed to be cheering him up!

Maybe things will get better soon. School is OK. The teachers are pretty good on the whole, the lessons are more interesting, and the kids aren't too bad. Renee now includes me in her group and I hang around with them. I hear about all the latest movies I haven't seen and all the rock groups I've never heard of. It's a real education. Trisha, the girl down the hall, is really nice but she's also really busy, with tons of homework and a job every evening. Maybe that's a good thing because I just don't feel ready to open up to strangers yet. I'm not even ready for new friends. I like to have people to eat lunch with, but that's all right now!

I realized later that I would have saved myself a lot of heartache if I'd opened up to Trisha sooner. The times we did have serious talks together, I could see that she was very wise for her age and gave very good advice.

I found that out when we were walking to school together one morning.

"Do you have a dress yet for the dance?" she asked me.

"What dance?"

"Oh, I guess you haven't heard yet," she said. "We always have a big Valentine's Day formal at school. We make a big thing of Valentine's Day. We have a rally and a girl's football game with boy cheerleaders, lots of fun stuff, and then the dance at night."

"Oh," I said, turning this information over in my mind.

"Do you think your boyfriend will drive down for it?" she asked.

I sighed. "It's a long way," I said.

"You haven't seen too much of him lately, have you?" she asked.

Suddenly I needed someone to talk to. "I haven't seen him at all," I said. "It's basketball. The team keeps on winning, and Ted keeps on practicing. He never seems to have time for me."

Trisha nodded as if she understood. "It sounds to me like he wants to break up gently with you," she said. "I mean, if you were really crazy about someone, you'd make time for him, wouldn't you?"

"I would," I said. "I wouldn't put a dumb old game ahead of anyone I loved."

"I don't want to interfere, but maybe you should let go," Trisha said slowly. "I mean, romance doesn't really work well at long distances. It's not fair to expect him to think about you when there are girls around him in school every day. You're not being fair to yourself, either. It only hurts more to keep on hoping all the time—and to shut yourself off from all the kids down here. There are some nice boys at school, you know. You're pretty—you'd find a date in no time at all, if you wanted one."

"But I don't want one," I blurted out. "I don't want to fit in down here. All I want is to be back home again, at my old school with Ted."

"That's pretty obvious," Trisha said. "We're not blind, you know. You're polite, but that's about all. You just stop short of being rude."

"Oh," I said, feeling my face turning red. I hadn't realized what I was feeling was so obvious.

Trisha reached out and touched my arm. "Look," she said, "I know it's never easy to move to a new high school, but you should try. I don't want to sound like I'm preaching, but you really could have a good time here, if you'd give us a try."

"But don't you see?" I said. "I don't want to get involved with people here and then have all the hurt if we move again."

"Are you planning to move again?"

I shrugged my shoulders. "My dad's getting better. He went out for a long walk yesterday. His doctor wants him to take up jogging in the spring."

Trisha looked at me steadily. "I know what you're thinking," she said. "You keep hoping that he'll be well enough to go back to ranching, don't you? Eden, you know that's not going to happen."

"Don't say that," I snapped at her. "Miracles have happened. It might!" And I strode ahead of her into school.

She didn't try to talk to me like that again, and I withdrew back into my shell.

Ted phoned a few days later. He sounded just as he always had, warm and funny and

58

loving. But when I asked him about the Valentine's formal, he turned very quiet. "That's an awful long way to drive for a dance," he said. "I mean, it's not your prom or anything. Don't get me wrong, I'd like to be with you, Eden, but not at your new school. I wouldn't know anybody, and I'd feel out of place down there. You understand, don't you?"

"So you don't mind if I go without you?" I asked, trying to stop my voice from quavering.

The line was quiet for a moment. But when he answered I could feel my daydreams being shattered. "Er, no, sure, go ahead. You don't want to miss out on all the fun, just because I'm not around." Another pause. Then, "Look, Eden, I really like you. But we're not engaged or anything. You understand what I'm saying?"

"Sure," I mumbled, trying to hold back the tears forming behind my eyes. "You're saying that you don't want me as your girlfriend anymore."

"It's not like that," he said quickly. "You really are special to me, but we're so far apart now. I don't want you to feel that you have to sit around waiting for me to show up. And I want to be free to take other girls to parties, too. In fact, I've asked Mary Alice to the basketball dance. I didn't think you'd mind."

After he had hung up I sat staring at the phone. *Good old Mary Alice, my old buddy,* I thought angrily. *Not only does she get my horse and my saddle, now she gets my boy-friend, too.* Probably forever, although part of me still wanted to hold on to the dream of our being together again someday. Nevertheless, when I went to bed that night I took off the silver chain I'd worn constantly since my birthday.

At school the next day it seemed as if everyone was talking about the dance. In every classroom girls were discussing what dresses they were going to wear and how they were going to do their hair. I couldn't help feeling a little jealous and left out, and so when I ran into Renee and her group after school, I was almost tempted to let her help me. I told her my boyfriend couldn't come down for the dance after all.

"That's too bad," she said. "You know you really should come without him. You'd meet lots of people and have a lot of fun."

"I bet you could find a nice date for Eden," Paula added.

"What about Mark?" Renee suggested. "You've met him, haven't you, Eden? You know, the really tall guy who's on the ski racing team?"

"He's cute, Eden," Paula agreed. "And he's a lot of fun, too. Why don't you let Renee ask him if he'll come with you?"

"Yeah, Eden," Kathy agreed. "We could go out shopping for a dress together. We know all the best places to buy clothes, and Renee goes to this great hairstylist."

"That's right," Renee agreed. "Tazi is really unique. She's a bit expensive for every day, but for a big occasion like this, she's really worth it. I bet she could do a wonderful French braid for your hair!" She gathered up my hair and swept it back. "Don't you think a French braid would be perfect for her?" she asked the girls.

Suddenly I began to panic. *What am I doing?* I asked myself. *I can't afford new dresses and hairstyles. I don't even want to go to this dance. How can I talk to a guy on the ski racing team?* I had this vision of myself, stammering and stuttering as I tried to pretend I knew something about skiing. I had another vision of myself trying to bluff my way out of buying a hundred-dollar dress or getting my hair done at a fancy salon.

"Look, guys, I really can't come to the dance," I said.

They all turned to look at me in amazement. "Why not?" Renee asked.

I groped around inside my head for an idea. "My boyfriend," I said at last. "He's the jealous type. He'd get really mad if I went without him."

"Let him get jealous, " Renee said with a grin. "Maybe he'll appreciate you more and come down for the next dance."

"I'd feel strange going behind his back," I said.

Paula giggled. "We're not fixing you up with someone to marry," she said. "It's only a dance. It's about time you had some fun down here. You haven't even been to any parties yet."

"Oh, and speaking of parties," Renee added, "there's a big one at my house after the dance. It usually goes on all night."

"I don't think my folks would let me party all night," I said hurriedly, glad that I finally had come up with a real excuse. "We're kind of old-fashioned back in Wyoming."

"Good old Wyoming," Renee said, grinning. "I bet a hoedown in the barn was the biggest thing there!"

The other girls laughed. "And they probably still have to have a chaperone to go courting," Paula added.

"And if your father sees you dancing with a strange guy, he freaks out!"

"He has a heart attack on the spot!" Renee clutched at her heart and made gasping noises.

They burst into wild laughter. I had been getting more and more angry as they made fun of my old home. Suddenly the anger spilled over.

"You'd better shut up. You're talking about things you know nothing about!" I yelled. "You don't know a thing about Wyoming. It's a great place full of real people. Not phonies like you. And you don't know a thing about heart attacks, either!"

Then I pushed past them and ran all the way home.

Chapter Eight

The wind coming in from the Rockies stung my face and snatched my breath away, but I didn't care. I just kept on running. The speed reminded me of galloping home on Charlie, feeling the wind in my face and my skin all tingly. Before I could stop myself I started wondering about Charlie, wondering whether Mary Alice was taking good care of him, whether her little brother Jason was hitting or kicking him when he wouldn't go.

"Oh, Charlie," I said out loud, "I miss you so much." Then I wondered if he still remembered me. That was the most painful thought of all, a picture in my mind of Charlie, raising his head as I came into his paddock and then going back to grazing again, not recognizing me.

It was my mom's day off, and my parents were both watching TV as I let myself in.

"Well, don't you look like the picture of health," my father said, greeting me. "You haven't had nice rosy cheeks like that for a long while."

"That's because I ran home," I said.

"Well, guess what? We may have taken the first step toward getting back on our feet today," my father said. He looked pleased with himself for the first time in weeks. "Your mother and I went out looking at storefronts to rent."

"And we've come up with a perfect little store near your school," my mother added.

"In that new complex?" I asked.

"Oh, no, not with those rents," my mother said. "It's in that pretty block with the Italian restaurant."

My mind moved quickly from the gleaming steel and glass to the run-down side street with the Italian restaurant.

"The realtor said it's in an up-and-coming area of town," my father added. "They're doing a lot of remodeling there now. Could be a good investment if the area becomes fashionable, and right now there isn't a decent hardware store in the neighborhood."

"So we'd go on living here?" I asked.

"That's the good thing," my mother said, smiling excitedly. "There's a nice big apartment over the store with a beautiful kitchen, all very modern. It's rented now, but if it becomes vacant, we might be able to move into it."

I looked from one face to the next. They were both smiling contentedly, as if everything were right with the world.

"So I guess you're both happy," I blurted out, anger spilling over like boiling milk.

The smiles faded from their faces. "Eden, what's wrong?" my father asked.

"It's just that nobody considers me or what *I* want." I knew I sounded like a spoiled brat, but I couldn't help myself.

"But we do consider you, sweetheart," my mother said. "Your father insisted on this place because you wouldn't have to change schools again."

"Maybe I *want* to change schools," I said. "Maybe I hate my school!"

"But you seemed to be doing so nicely," my father said. "You've never complained."

"Maybe I should have complained earlier. Maybe if I'd made a great big fuss at Thanksgiving we never would have left Wyoming!"

"Eden!" my mother said sharply. "You know there was no way we could have kept the ranch!"

"That's what *you* kept telling me," I yelled. "And now I see why. You're quite happy with your new job. That's all you wanted in life, and now you've got it!"

"Eden, I won't have you talking to your mother like that!" my father said, rising from his chair.

"Jake, sit down, this isn't good for your heart," my mother interrupted.

"It's always his heart, his heart," I shouted. "Doesn't anybody ever think that my heart has been broken a million times over?"

I swallowed down a sob, wrenched open our front door, and ran down the hall. I could hear them shouting after me, but I didn't wait. All I wanted to do was get outside and run and run until I could make myself forget. Or ride. If only Charlie were there right then.

After three blocks of running full out, I stopped, gasping for breath as I leaned against a phone booth. The blast of cold air in my face had brought me down to earth again. I felt very ashamed of my outburst. If only I could explain to my parents that my nerves were stretched to the snapping point. If they'd known how I felt about the dance and about giving up Charlie, they would have understood. If only I'd still had Charlie, I could have galloped for miles over the hills and then I would have felt much better.

Right then I knew exactly what I wanted to do. I had to ride.

Slight problem of no horse, I reminded myself. *But there must be stables, even around a city.* I went into the phone booth and opened the yellow pages. There were several stables listed. One even called itself a riding academy. That was obviously going to cost a fortune. One was way on the other side of town. A third, Bradley's Trail Rides, sounded more hopeful, and I knew the bus that went out to that suburb.

Ten minutes later I was sitting in the over-heated bus, watching rows of suburban houses flash by. I finally got off in the no-man's-land between city and country. There were poultry coops outside a few houses, and I noticed a few horses standing around a bale of hay. I also spotted a lot full of wrecked car parts, looking like modern sculpture peeping through the snow. A pile of old tires made a neat little mountain in one yard.

Then I saw the sign, "Bradley's Horses for Hire," tacked up beside a fence. The gate was shut and I realized then that they might be closed on a winter afternoon. But nothing was going to stop me, so I opened the gate and went inside.

The first thing that hit me was the smell. I'd grown up on a ranch. I'd cleaned out Charlie's stall and been in the cow barn where we kept the calves in winter, but I'd never smelled anything that bad. I found myself coughing and sneezing. Looking around, I realized I was standing in a small yard with stable doors on both sides.

I walked over to the nearest door and opened it. The smell was so bad it made my eyes smart. About ten horses were lined up, tethered to rings on the wall, shifting uncomfortably on the piles of manure that had built up beneath their feet. The feed racks in front of them were mostly empty, but the horses were not overly thin. It just looked as if nobody had taken care of them in a while.

As I turned to walk out into the fresh air again I heard a voice yelling behind me. "Hey, you! What do you think you're doing here?"

An enormous old man came hobbling toward me. He was so big he looked like a bad giant in a cartoon. His old flannel jacket was so dirty that I could no longer see the color of the plaid. A tattered Denver Broncos wool hat was perched on top of his head, and a cigarette hung out of the corner of his mouth, twitching up and down as he spoke.

Every single thing that had happened to me all day had made me feel angrier and angrier. Now this was the last straw. It seemed so unfair that I should have no horse of my own, when this crummy, revolting old man should have all the horses in the world. I stepped bravely toward him.

"I thought there were supposed to be horses for hire here," I said.

He looked at me as if I were crazy. "I only do trail rides on the weekends in winter," he said.

"I don't want a trail ride," I said. "I want a horse."

"I don't hire out horses," he said. "Only on trail rides. Don't want some stupid kid pretending he's the Lone Ranger or something and breaking my horses' legs."

He came closer until he towered over me,

smelling not too good himself. I was scared, but I was angry, too.

"Is that so?" I asked furiously. "Well, for your information, I bet I ride better than anyone else around here. I have enough blue ribbons from shows to paper a wall. And another thing, if you care so much about your horses breaking their legs, how come you let them live in such disgusting surroundings? You ought to be ashamed of yourself, keeping poor horses like that. I've a good mind to report you to the Humane Society!"

I suddenly realized that I was yelling at a man who probably weighed three hundred pounds and that I was all alone in the middle of nowhere. My voice trailed off and I stepped back. But instead of shouting back at me, the man just laughed.

"Little fighter, aren't you?" he said. He put his hand up and scratched the thatch of gray hair that stuck out from under his cap. For a while he continued looking at me in silence.

"You ever take care of your own horse?" he asked.

"Of course I did," I said. "Perfectly."

He smiled. "Ever try taking care of *twenty-five* horses all by yourself?" he asked. "That's not so easy, especially when you've got arthritis and some days you just can't lift your arms."

"Then why don't you hire someone to help you?" I asked.

He snorted. "Don't make any money in the

winter," he said. "I can barely afford to feed my horses. In the summer it's fine. All the kids come down and help, and the horses more or less pay for themselves."

"I'll tell you what," I heard myself saying, "I'll come down and help you after school—on condition you let me ride the horses and you pay me when you can afford to."

He stared at me again, taking a slow puff on his cigarette.

"Young lady," he said at last, "you just got yourself a job."

Chapter Nine

It was only on the bus ride home that I realized what I'd done.

"Have you totally lost your mind?" I asked myself, staring at my reflection in the dark glass of the window. "You've just agreed to work for no pay for the most horrible old man in Denver. It'll take forever to clean out those stalls and get those horses looking respectable again—and he won't thank you for it, either. He'll just make you work and then he probably won't even let you ride."

I half decided to call him as soon as I got home and tell him I'd changed my mind. But then I thought of all those poor horses standing in their filth and decided to give it a try.

As I walked up the dark street toward our block, I remembered how I had run out of the house after that ugly fight. Now I hesitated to go back. Before we moved here I had hardly ever fought with my parents. I had never said the sort of mean, spiteful things I'd said that day. I didn't even know why I'd done it. I knew how hard things were for them. It couldn't have been easy for my mother to start a new job and meet lots of strange people, working long hours while she was worrying all the time about my father. I knew it wasn't easy for Dad staying home while she went out to work. Now they'd both seemed excited about the store they wanted to open, and I'd spoiled it for them.

I walked up and down the block awhile, looking in store windows at clothes I couldn't afford until I decided that I was so cold and hungry anything would be better than staying out on the street.

"Eden, where have you been?" my mother demanded as soon as I let myself in. "We've been worried sick about you."

"I'm sorry, but I needed to get away," I said. "I decided to go out to a riding school and look for a job."

"You might have told us first," my mother said. "I made Dad go and rest, he was getting so worked up."

"Is that Eden?" I heard Dad's voice from the bedroom. He shuffled out in his bedroom slippers, looking like an old man. I was sorry I'd made him worry. It seemed that everything I did was wrong these days.

"Thank heavens you're back safely," he said, coming over and putting his arms around me. "We couldn't think where you'd gone."

"I'm sorry I made you worry. I just had to get away."

"I understand, honey," he said. "We talked about it after you left. We realized how hard this has been on you, but it's got to start getting better soon. We have to believe that—"

"Eden went out to get a job at a riding school," my mother interrupted.

My father's face broke into a big grin. "Hey, that's terrific, Eden. Did you get it?"

"Yes," I said.

"Good girl," he said, hugging me harder. "That's my girl. I knew you'd come through all right."

"Hey, it's not as good as all that," I said. "I mean, I'm not getting paid. But I get to ride, and he really needs the help. You should see the horses—they were disgusting. He's an old man, and he's been trying to take care of them by himself because he can't afford to hire anyone."

"It'll do you good to be around horses again," my father said. "Maybe by summer he'll give you a proper job and pay you regularly."

"You do need something to keep you occupied after school," Mom said. She sighed, then walked through to the kitchen and opened the oven. "Here, come and sit down. I've been keeping your dinner warm." She put a plate of stew on the table. The wonderful, rich, warm smell wafted over me. I sat down and started eating.

The next day I dreaded going to school and facing all the girls. I hoped that maybe I could slink around invisibly and spend lunch hour in the library. But as I opened my locker to put away my homework, Renee appeared right behind me.

"Er, look, Eden," she said, in a voice surprisingly quiet for her. "About yesterday—we had no idea about your father. I just found out that he'd really had a heart attack. I'm sorry we said all those dumb things."

"It's OK," I mumbled.

"So we're still friends?" Renee asked. "And you'll come to the dance?"

"I don't think I'll come to the dance," I said. "But I'd still like to be friends."

"Great," Renee said, smiling as if she understood. "Look, Eden, we kid around a lot in our group and say a lot of things we don't mean. It's just teasing. It means you're one of us."

"We used to kid around at my old school," I said. "I don't mind it, honestly."

"If you want to come over and do homework after school someday—" Renee began.

"Thanks," I mumbled. "But I've got an after-school job."

"Oh, doing what?"

"Helping out at a riding stable," I said.

Renee wrinkled her nose. "Better you than me," she said. "I guess all that manure makes you feel at home."

That time I could laugh with her.

After school I went home and changed into my old riding jeans, then caught the bus out to Bradley's. Mr. Bradley was sitting on an old chair in his office—a very polite description for an extra horse stall with a beat-up table, chair, and oil heater in it. He had an ashtray full of cigarette stubs in front of him, and another cigarette hung from his lip. He looked up as I peered in through the window.

"Well, what do you know?" he said, rising to his feet and filling that small space like an inflating balloon. "I didn't think you'd show up again."

"Why not?" I asked. "I said I would."

"There's a lot of difference between what people say and what they do," he said. "And these city kids, they think it'd be such fun to have a horse of their own—until they try to take care of it, that is. You didn't look like the sort of girl who'd want to shovel out manure."

"For your information," I said frostily, "I grew up on a cattle ranch in Wyoming where I lived until about six weeks ago. There's nothing to do with animals that I haven't done."

"Is that so?" he asked, looking slightly impressed for the first time. "Well, maybe you'll be some use to me after all. What do you want to do first?"

"What needs doing most?"

He snorted, sounding like a horse himself. "Everything. You name one thing that doesn't need doing. I don't have a pasture—just the one little field behind and that's only big enough for about five horses. I rotate them out there, and the rest of them have to stay in the stalls. Makes a lot of mess that way."

I was glad to hear that the horses got a chance to stretch their legs occasionally. "OK," I said, walking out into the yard again. "I'll start by cleaning out some stalls, then maybe do some grooming before it gets dark." I paused. "Then perhaps I'll be able to take out one of the horses?"

"Let's see how good you are at working first," he said. "Come on. The light won't last forever."

He walked me around the yard, showing me where the shovels were kept, where the tack room was, where the feed was stored. "And there's the wheelbarrow," he said. "Now get on with it."

With that he turned and shuffled back toward his office. "And a Merry Christmas to you, too, Mr. Scrooge," I muttered, throwing a shovel into the wheelbarrow and dragging it over the rutted surface toward the closest row of stalls. Unlike the big stable across the yard, these were individual boxes, containing only one horse apiece. I cleaned out one, delighted to be close to a real, living horse again, to feel her hot steamy breath snorting on the back of my neck as I bent down. The horse seemed glad to see me, too, nudging up against me and standing in a happy trance as I scratched behind her ears. She was such a gentle little mare that I just had to stop to brush her down and get the tangles out of her too-long coat. "Maybe I'll even take you out later," I told her.

She looked at me longingly as I closed the door. I could tell she was thinking that my visit wasn't real, that I was sort of a horse fairy godmother who was about to vanish into thin air.

"I'll be back, promise," I said, laughing at her big mournful eyes.

I was in a good mood by the time I opened the next door. Just being around horses again made me feel that I had been asleep for months and just woken up. I swung open the next door.

"Here comes the cleaning service," I said brightly. I had a sudden impression of a flash of gold as hooves reared up at me. Quickly I flung myself backward and forced the door closed.

"Mr. Bradley!" I yelled. He came shuffling out of his room, scowling at me.

"What is it this time?" he asked, even though there hadn't been a time before.

"You might have told me you have a killer

behind that door," I said. "I nearly got a hoof in my face."

His face broke into a big, ugly laugh. "Oh, yes. Old King. I'd forgotten about him. He can be mean with strangers."

"I don't think that's very funny," I said. "That's a dangerous horse."

"Don't I know it," he said. "Worst investment I ever made. But then you take a look at him. What would you have done if you were me?" He went over to King's stall and opened the top half of the door. The horse gave a terrifying snort and thrust his head out. I had to gasp, because I was looking at one of the most beautiful horses I had ever seen. He was a big horse, but his face was as delicate as a thoroughbred's. His coat looked as if it were made of spun gold, and the mane that cascaded down almost looked like pure silver. Even among champions at a horse show I would have noticed him. To find him there, in that dirty little stable yard, was a miracle.

Mr. Bradley looked at my face and laughed again. "Pretty, ain't he?" he said. "That's what I thought when I bought him last summer. I got him up at a sale in Montana. I needed new horses like a hole in the head, but how could I refuse this one? Of course, when I got him home I realized why he was so cheap. He'd come from a roundup of wild stallions, and they'd never been able to properly break him. So now I'm stuck with a useless, good-looking horse. I can't put my trail

79

customers on him. Even the experienced ones can't control the son-of-a-gun. A leaf flutters in front of his face and he runs for it! I tried him myself a couple of times, and I don't consider myself a weak man, but I couldn't stop him when he wanted to go."

"So what's going to happen to him?" I asked. Those beautiful brown eyes were looking at me calmly now. Bravely I walked across to him and started to stroke his nose. He stood there quietly, accepting the stroking.

"You tell me," Mr. Bradley said. "I run an ad in the paper every now and then, hoping I can sell him to a bigger sucker than me! If not, I guess he goes for dog meat."

King got bored with my stroking and tossed up his head, skittering around inside his stall. The temptation to prove to myself that I could ride him and to show Mr. Bradley I was no slouch was overwhelming.

"He's been cooped up too long," I said. "Look how skittish he is. Why don't you let me take him out and exercise him?"

Mr. Bradley laughed a great booming laugh. "He'd make mincemeat of you, girl," he said.

"My horse was about the same size as him," I said. "He hated to jump, but I trained him to be one of the best jumpers in the state."

Mr. Bradley looked me slowly up and down, and a smile that looked sarcastic spread across his face. "OK. Go ahead then," he said. "Personally, I wouldn't take him out on a frosty afternoon after he'd been kept inside all week, but you're the expert. Go ahead."

He stood there watching me while I brought out tack. I slipped the bridle over King's head, then led him out and handed Mr. Bradley the reins before he could object. With Mr. Bradley holding the reins it wasn't too hard to throw the saddle onto his back, and though he danced about when I tried to tighten the girth, he didn't try to kick me again.

By the time he was saddled he looked even bigger than ever—much taller than Charlie, I had to admit. I'd really have liked a leg up onto his back, but I wanted Mr. Bradley to see what an experienced rider I was. So I let down the stirrup, took a deep breath, and swung myself up into the saddle. Mr. Bradley let go of the reins and stepped back safely out of the way. I collected the reins rapidly and at first King danced around in circles, tucking his head in, fighting against the bit. When I figured he had relaxed a little, I urged him forward. Charlie had always been a stubborn old thing and had needed a good kick to get him going. I gave this horse the same sort of command, but he took off much faster than I had intended.

" 'Bye, Mr. Bradley. I'll be back in a little while," I yelled, trying to appear completely in control of the situation as we clattered out of the gate.

It was clear to me that King had been inside much too long so I let him go at his own pace, pounding down the grass beside the road with his giant strides. He was a very smooth ride with almost no up and down movement, but I could feel the raw, untamed power beneath me.

We reached a crossroads and he reined in perfectly to a stop. I turned King to the left, where the real country started, and we thundered away.

I guess Mr. Bradley doesn't know as much about riding as he thinks, I decided as the trail wound its way between the trees. *I bet he brings a whip and spurs with him and uses them to make a horse go.*

The land started to rise into the first hint of hills I had seen. We followed the trail up until we could look down on the city. I could see rows of taillights making red ribbons along the highway and lights already winking through the wintry haze.

"I guess we'd better be getting back, King," I said. "We don't want to be caught too far away in the dark."

As I turned him toward the stable, a jackrabbit suddenly shot across the trail. King neighed in alarm and sprang forward, his ears flat against his head.

"Whoa, King. Easy, boy," I called, leaning over to pat his neck. He ignored me. We were going faster and faster. The snow flew up as we plunged down the narrow trail. I was using all my strength on the reins, trying to pull his head in, but it was like pulling at solid rock. The trees loomed up before us and suddenly branches were flashing by, snatching and scratching at me. I bent low over his neck, no longer trying to stop him, only to stay on and not get knocked off by a branch.

Suddenly I saw an enormous fir tree ahead of us. The path divided and went around it. King was heading straight for the tree. He skidded to a halt just in time and reared up, dancing on his hind legs while he waved his forelegs in the air.

"It's OK, King. Easy, boy, easy," I crooned. He landed back on all four legs and stood there, trembling. I was shaking pretty badly, too, but I patted him and talked to him until we set off again, this time at a gentle walk.

"So how was the ride?" Mr. Bradley asked when we got back. "Any broken bones?"

"I didn't fall, if that's what you mean," I said, sliding from King's back and leading him toward his stall. "He moves beautifully," I added. "He runs like the wind."

"Well, how about that," Mr. Bradley said, leaning on the stable gate and watching me as I took off King's saddle and rubbed him down. "I never thought I'd see the day when a little skinny girl could do something I can't do. You must be some rider, Eden. If you can work on him till you beat the devil out of him once and for all, I can ask any money I want for him and get it. It was a lucky day for me when you came here!" He shuffled away, chuckling to himself.

That should have been my moment of victory. I had scored the winning point against a man I despised. Instead I felt a tight knot of fear. Until that day I had thought I was a pretty hot rider. Now I knew I wasn't so great after all. I had let a horse run away with me. I hadn't been strong enough to control him. Maybe I still had a thing or two to learn.

Chapter Ten

As I lay in bed that night, half awake and listening to the city sounds below me, I went over that ride with King in my mind. I could see the trees flashing past me and feel my hands burning from the leather reins cutting into them. As I drifted into sleep, I kept pulling harder and harder on them, but the horse wouldn't stop.

I had never been scared of a horse before. Even when I was a tiny girl and my father would put me on the back of our neighbor's big workhorse I wasn't frightened. I'd just kick his enormous back with my little girl's shoes until he lumbered into an ungainly trot. Charlie had thrown me off enough times, especially when I first started teaching him to jump. I'd gotten bruised and battered and even had to have stitches in my arm once after I fell over a gate, but I'd never been scared to get back on again.

But I was scared of King. He was too strong for me, and he knew it. He would always know it, and anytime he felt like running away with me, he would. Yet Mr. Bradley wanted me to get him licked into shape.

By the time I reached the stables the next day, the weather had worsened. The mountains to the west were blotted out behind a threatening bank of clouds, and a stinging sleet was starting to fall.

"Here she is, my champion rider," Mr. Bradley greeted me as I came in through the gate. "All set for another session?"

"You don't really expect me to take King out today, do you?" I asked. "The weather's terrible."

"Oh, horses don't even notice the weather," he said.

"But I do," I answered. "I'm not going to catch pneumonia riding in this weather. Besides, if it rains, then ices over, it'll be dangerous."

"Maybe you're right," he said. "Too bad, though. I want you to get King in shape for the spring sales. If you can turn him into a nice quiet horse, I'll make a fortune on him!"

"And what about me?" I retorted. "What do I get out of it?"

"Don't worry, girl. You'll get your share," he said. "I'll pay you ten percent. And I tell you what—you want to lead my trail rides this weekend? I'll give you ten bucks a time for those."

"OK," I said. Leading a trail ride sounded nice and peaceful compared to breaking a half-wild stallion.

The weather stayed bad for the next couple of days, so I worked around the stable yard. On Saturday morning the sky was as clear as glass, and I left for the stable right after breakfast. By this time the stables were all clean and the horses well groomed.

"Good to see you occupied again," my father said as I was pulling on my boots, ready to leave that Saturday.

"And guess what, Dad," I said, in a voice much brighter than it had been lately. "Bradley's paying me ten dollars for each ride I lead on weekends."

A smile crossed his face. "That'll soon add up," he said. He walked across to the window and stared out at the blue arc of sky behind the buildings. "If I were you, I'd even pay him for the chance to be out on a horse this morning," he said. "If only I . . ." Then he let the drape fall across the window and walked slowly back to his chair.

My heart ached for him at that moment. I wanted to go over and hug him and tell him that he could go back to being his old self again. But I couldn't lie. And I really couldn't think of anything to say to make him feel better. Blowing him a kiss, I tiptoed out the door.

"Good clear morning," Mr. Bradley said, greeting me. "This will bring them out of the woodwork, you wait and see. Better saddle me up ten horses to begin with. If we need more, we'll saddle them later."

One by one I led the horses out, saddled them up, and tied them to the rail. The horses snorted appreciatively in the crisp air, their steaming breath making them look like a row of tied dragons. King poked his head out of his box and watched with interest.

I didn't have much more time to think because people started arriving: excited little girls all dressed up in new riding outfits, fussy mothers inspecting the horses and deciding which ones looked safe, older kids who greeted the horses like long lost friends, and a few adults who looked around nervously.

Mr. Bradley appeared like magic to take money from everyone and matched up people and horses so firmly that nobody dared to argue. At last everyone was mounted, and the little mare, Jessie, was standing waiting for me. Mr. Bradley went over the route and the rules with me once more, muttering under his breath about which riders were likely to give me trouble.

I went among the riders, giving girths a final check, making sure beginners knew how to hang on to the saddle horn. Then the gate opened again, and a tall, athletic-looking boy strolled in. He was wearing black cords and a black ski jacket, which contrasted sharply with the perfectly styled, pale blond hair that framed his untanned face. He looked around with a proud, angry stare, like a prince who'd come to inspect the peasants.

"Boy, what a dump," I heard him mutter. He looked around some more and saw me. "You work here?" he demanded. "How do I go about hiring a horse?"

"We have a trail ride leaving in a few minutes," I said. "But I think it's full."

"I don't want to ride along with a lot of little kids," he said haughtily. "And I don't want one of these tired, broken-down old horses. Find me something with spirit, will you?"

I was very tempted to tell him that I was the only thing around there with spirit and then throw him out. We stared at each other like two boxers climbing into the ring. He looked so pleased with himself that I regretted having cleaned up the stable yard so well. If there'd been a pile of manure behind him, I would have made him step backward.

"You're looking at the only horses we have," I said frostily. "And right now they're all taken."

"That one doesn't look too bad," he said, pointing at Jessie, who was already saddled for me. "At least that one doesn't look as if it'll die on me before we leave the yard!"

"That happens to be my horse," I said.

"Ride something else," he demanded.

"We have nothing left except two very small ponies," I said. "And I don't intend to jog along beside everyone."

For an instant I saw a smile flash across his face, then it froze back into the proud, scornful stare. "Maybe I'd better talk to your boss," he said.

"You're welcome to," I said. "But you'd rather deal with me than with him. He has a terrible temper."

"I'll risk it," he said. "I took the trouble to come down here and ride, and I'm not leaving until I do."

"Fine," I said. "I'll get the boss for you."

Mr. Bradley came waddling out at the sound of his name. "What is it now?" he roared so fiercely that two little kids clutched their mothers. But the boy didn't bat an eyelid.

"I want to hire a horse, and your stablegirl here can't seem to find me one," he said, stepping toward Mr. Bradley.

Mr. Bradley eyed his expensive outfit. "Why can't we find him a horse?" he growled at me.

"The ride's full except for Jessie, and I have to ride something," I said.

"I don't want to go on a ride," the boy interrupted. "I just want to hire out a horse. A nice, lively horse, OK?"

"Not OK," Mr. Bradley said. "I don't hire

out horses until I've seen how a person can ride. You can take the mare that's saddled over there and join the ride if you want."

"And what do I ride?" I demanded. "Or do you want me to walk?"

He looked around. "Saddle up King."

"King?" I blurted out with disbelief. "You want me to lead a ride on King?"

"Oh, he's fine with other horses," he said calmly. "They know he's boss and he knows it. No trouble that way at all. The trail's nice and gentle. Good advertisement for the stables, too, to see a horse like that leading the ride."

Before I could protest further, Mr. Bradley walked to King's box and put on the bridle. I kept trying to think of something to say that would get me out of this gracefully. I was not going to admit I was scared in front of all those people, especially not that boy. He had walked over to King's stable behind us. I didn't know he was there until he spoke.

"Oh, I think I'll take that horse instead," he said. "He looks much better than yours."

I turned to find myself staring into the brightest blue eyes I'd ever seen.

Go ahead, take him, I thought. But Mr. Bradley spoke before me. "I'd have to see what kind of a rider you are before you take a horse like King," he said. "Only the most experienced rider can handle him. This young lady's won dozens of blue ribbons and cups

91

and things. She can handle him, but not many other people can."

Again I was aware of the blue eyes sizing me up, looking at me critically. "Oh, I didn't realize I was in the presence of an expert," he said. A sarcastic smile passed his lips. For an instant my eyes met his, then he turned and walked over to Jessie.

Mr. Bradley held King while I swung myself up. "Don't let that kid get away with anything," he muttered as he adjusted my stirrup. "We get his type a lot. Think they know everything."

I didn't really see how I could stop a boy twice my size from getting away with anything, but I didn't say that to Mr. Bradley. Actually I was too worried about riding King again to form any coherent thoughts. I could feel my stomach start to clench into a tight knot. *Why am I doing this?* I kept asking myself. *I'll just tell him I don't want to ride King, and if he doesn't like it I'll go home. Simple as that.*

But it wasn't really as simple as that. A whole group of people were watching me. I could see the respect on their faces as King danced in circles. Mr. Bradley thought I was a top rider. Somehow at the moment it seemed better to take a chance on King than to look like a fool in front of them—especially the boy. I glanced over and noticed him watching me, with a cool, almost amused stare.

You can't control him half as well as I

could, those eyes seemed to be saying. In that instant I knew that there was no way I was going to admit defeat. I was going to lead that ride on King, whatever happened!

Chapter Eleven

We started out in a long line and headed up a trail that twisted through a nearby state park. Once we had left the main road behind there was total silence, except for the crunch of the horses' hooves on the snowy grass and an occasional snort somewhere at the back of the line. I didn't look back but I was very conscious of that boy. Why did he have to show up right then? It was his fault I was on an enormous horse I couldn't control properly. He was the rudest, most arrogant person I had ever met. The trouble was that he was also so incredibly good-looking that I couldn't stop thinking about him. *The only person I've met in almost two months that I'm attracted to*, I thought angrily, *and he has to be the most obnoxious person in Den-*

ver! Well, I'm not going to make a fool of myself today, whatever happens. He'll see how a good rider handles a horse like this!

So I kept King well reined in and he danced along patiently at the front of the line, seeming to realize that we had to move at a snail's pace. I also kept a good lookout for falling leaves, jackrabbits, fire trucks, and anything else that might spook him. That day I wanted to be one step ahead of him.

We wound our way through the trees. Apart from one little girl's horse who wanted to stop and eat every blade of grass he saw, we had no major problems. Bare grasslands sprinkled with snow in places stretched just ahead of us. I turned back to the other riders.

"Please stay in line," I said. "We have to keep to the trail. Don't let your horses stop and eat;it's not good for them. Just pull their heads up very firmly if they try to put them down and give them a good kick at the same time."

"Won't that hurt him?" the little girl asked, reaching down to pat her fat pony's side.

I smiled. "There's no way you could kick him hard enough to make it hurt," I said. "You have to show him who's boss, or he'll hold us all up."

"When do we get to go a bit faster?" a voice beside me said. It was the boy, who had moved up beside me on Jessie. King sidestepped nervously, and I tightened my hold on him.

"We don't," I answered coldly. "These are mostly beginners. Besides, the ground is icy."

"Why don't you and I just go ahead for a while?" he asked. "Just one quick gallop? I can see your horse is dying to get moving." He flashed me a smile that suddenly transformed his whole face. Before he had looked bad-tempered, spoiled, and sulky. The smile was almost like switching on a lightbulb. His whole face lit up.

I fought against being influenced by the smile. "I can't just desert these people and gallop ahead," I said. "All these other horses would try to follow, and we'd have people falling off." His grin widened. "Besides," I said, trying to sound like somebody who was in command of things, "my horse is only dancing around because you're too close to him."

"Smart horse," the boy said, his smile now switched off. "He's got the right attitude. Keep everyone away, then you won't get kicked." He flashed me a challenging glance. "What would you do if I went ahead alone?" he asked. "Would you leave all your little charges and come after me?"

"I'd let you gallop over the nearest cliff," I blurted out sarcastically. "Go ahead and break your neck!"

"Well, in that case . . ." he said. Before I could stop him Jessie was streaking off down the trail.

"Come back here right now, you idiot!" I yelled. A couple of the other horses tried to follow. I headed them off, grabbing their reins and calming them down. "It's OK, everyone," I said, trying to sound as if this sort of thing happened every day. "Just keep a firm hold on your horses. We'll get him back in a second."

I stood there for a moment deciding whether to go after him to prevent anything from happening to Jessie or whether to stay to prevent anything from happening to the other people. I could see that Jessie was now moving at a flat-out gallop. It looked as if he had lost control of her, just as King had run away with me the other day.

Then my decision was taken away from me. The boy let out a tremendous whoop, and before I could do anything sensible, King leaped away after them.

Since King was a much bigger and stronger horse we flew over the ground, gaining on them with every stride. As soon as we drew level, the boy flashed me an excited smile.

"See, I knew I could get you to join me," he yelled.

"You must be crazy!" I yelled back. "Stop right now!"

We were racing side by side, both horses with their ears back and necks extended as if they were the leaders in the Kentucky Derby. I kept looking across at Jessie's reins, wondering if I could do a rodeo trick and bring his horse to a stop. The trouble was that I had no way of stopping King.

"This is fun!" he yelled back.

"It won't be when we both plunge over a cliff!" I shouted. "And it won't be fun when Mr. Bradley hears about it! He'll kill us both."

"You want me to stop?" he yelled again.

"Yes!"

"Oh, OK," he said. Instantly he jerked Jessie to a halt. I reined in hard on King, and luckily he skidded to a halt beside her.

"That was great," the boy said. "Now we can go back to the little kiddies."

Now that the two horses had actually stopped, I felt a new rush of anger rise up inside me.

"That was stupid!" I yelled at him. "Some of those other horses tried to follow you. Someone might have gotten killed, and it would have been your fault—only I would have gotten the blame because I'm in charge here. You don't know Mr. Bradley. He'll kill me when he hears about this."

"Oh, don't worry," he said smoothly. "I'll just tell him my horse bolted, and you very bravely raced after me and brought me to a stop. They give out medals for things like that! You ought to thank me."

He flashed his sarcastic smile again as he urged Jessie back toward the group.

"I hope you're not thinking of doing a dumb thing like this again before we get back," I said, bringing King up into step beside him.

"Oh, don't worry, I'll be a good boy from

now on," he said. "I've done what I wanted to do."

"And what was that?"

He looked rather smug as he turned to me. "To see what it felt like to gallop."

I looked at him slowly. "You've never galloped before?"

"I've never ridden before, period," he said.

I shook my head in disbelief. Then I laughed. "You're putting me on," I scoffed. "You ride as well as I do."

"Just natural talent," he said. "I do most things well. Correction, I *did* most things well." Suddenly his face went hard, and he urged his horse into a lope down the trail ahead of me.

After that the ride went on without incident. As we drew close to the stables, the boy drew Jessie level with me again. "Don't worry," he said, noticing my anxious look, "I'm not going to get too close, and I don't intend to gallop again. I've tried riding and it was fun, but not as challenging as I had thought."

"So you're going to give it up and move on to more exciting things?" I said. "Sky diving, maybe, or white-water rafting?"

"Maybe," he said seriously. "There's so much to do."

"And so little time to do it?" I asked jokingly.

"And so little time to do it," he said, staring out ahead of him.

We continued on, side by side, silent again, both lost in our own thoughts. The gallop had tired King nicely, so that I no longer felt as if I were sitting on a supercharged engine.

I found myself sneaking a glance at the boy beside me. His blond hair had fallen forward across his forehead, and he had a faraway look in his eyes, as if his thoughts had moved him to a place where no one could reach him. The proud, angry look was gone as he stared out ahead, not conscious of being watched. I wondered what had made him behave so rudely in the stable yard. Maybe he was one of those people who say the wrong thing when they're insecure or scared. I could relate to that very well indeed!

The boy must have sensed my eyes on him. He glanced over and gave me a quick smile.

"So," he said with almost forced cheerfulness. "Do you do this all the time?"

"I've just started," I said.

"Pretty boring job, isn't it?" he asked.

"I like riding," I said.

"I can't see the thrill in walking along with a bunch of tired old horses," he said. "That horse you're riding isn't too bad, I suppose. But there's no challenge, is there?"

"Are you kidding?" I asked. "He happens to be a wild stallion that nobody broke in properly. He's only behaving well today because I'm making him."

"Yeah, well, I could see he would be a bit of a handful for you," he said thoughtfully.

I shook my head in disbelief. "You think you know it all, don't you?" I demanded. "You ride a nice, gentle little mare once and think you know everything about riding. For your information the gallop is the easiest pace to ride, because it's so even. There's nothing smart about it at all. You should try an English canter over some fences."

"That might not be a bad idea," he said. "I'll try that tomorrow. You can come along and watch me if you like."

We'd reached the stables, and I stopped to lead the other horses into the yard. "Why would I want to watch you?" I demanded when I returned to the boy.

"Because you might learn something about riding," he said with a triumphant grin as he slid to the ground.

"Oh, expert," I said, smiling back calmly, "there's just one thing. You get off a horse on the left side, not the right!"

For a second his face flushed pink. I slipped down from King and led him away from the other horses.

"What are you looking so pleased about?" Mr. Bradley growled, taking King's reins from me.

"Oh, it's just nice to know that it takes awhile to become an expert," I said loudly enough to be overheard.

Chapter Twelve

When I got home there was a letter from Ted waiting for me. To say I was shocked was an understatement. I hadn't heard from him at all since I asked him to go to the dance with me. There was no mention of the dance in his letter, which was short and cheerful and full of impersonal news about teachers and classes and the basketball team. The closest he got to emotion was telling me how lost he was going to feel when basketball season was over. He said he didn't know what he'd do with his afternoons and then went on.

Oh, by the way, Mary Alice's brother is riding Charlie to school, just like you used to. She's going on the school trip to Washington during spring recess, and she's

trying to talk me into going. Do I look like the kind of guy who needs a big dose of politics? Hope to get down your way soon. Got to go.
Love,
Ted.

It wasn't a bad letter, but I sat there, folding and unfolding it for a while, wondering about things. Like why he'd written. It was hard to do, but finally I had to admit that things were over between us. Reading between the lines, I also got the impression that Mary Alice was his new girlfriend.

I thought about writing back, but decided it was better if I didn't. It was better for me to make a clean break and realize that Ted was now a part of my past.

Mom noticed my sad face. "The letter?" she asked hesitantly.

I shrugged. "Wyoming seems so far away now."

My father looked up from a tool catalog. "At least you've found some horses here."

"Did you get the old man to pay you?" my mother asked, changing the subject.

"I don't actually have the money yet," I admitted. "But if I lead two more rides tomorrow, I'll get forty bucks this weekend, which isn't bad."

"If he pays up," my mother said. "And if he doesn't, I think you ought to stop going there. There are plenty of ways to make money in this town. Your father will need help once he opens the store. You might want to help him in the afternoons."

She didn't understand at all. I opened my mouth to speak, but before I could say anything my father interrupted. "Leave her be, Maggie," he said gently. "The girl needs her fresh air and her horses. The money's not important in this case."

But I knew I shouldn't let Mr. Bradley get the better of me. I made a resolution that I wouldn't leave the stables the next day without my money.

Sunday was another lovely clear day. "Got a busy day ahead of you," Mr. Bradley greeted me, dropping ash down his checkered flannel shirt as he spoke. "One ride. Maybe two. And a private lesson."

"A private lesson?" I asked. "I didn't think you gave them."

"I'll do anything if the money's right," he said, grinning at me with his repulsive black teeth. "This kid Ryan especially requested a private lesson."

My mind painted a horrible picture of a spoiled little brat, dressed from head to toe in new riding clothes, with a nice leather whip in his hand, and a mommy wrapped up in mink against the cold, trotting along beside him to make sure he didn't fall off.

"So what am I supposed to do?" I asked.

"Teach the kid a thing or two," Mr. Bradley

grunted. "Now go get the horses saddled up before he arrives."

I was tightening Pixie's girth straps when a voice in my ear made me jump.

"Hi, Eden," it said. "Are you ready to go?"

I spun around, and there was my know-it-all gorgeous guy from the day before.

"What are you doing here?" I asked, feeling my cheeks turn pink even though I wanted to look cold and disinterested. "And how did you know my name?"

"I asked the old guy," he said. "Nice name. It reminds me of fig leaves and apples."

I managed to stop the blush and frowned at him. "I thought you gave up on horseback riding yesterday. Isn't today skydiving?"

He flashed me an angry look, and I could tell instantly that he hated to be teased. "I was thinking about it last night," he said, "and I realized that I might still have a thing or two to learn. Besides, I want to try a horse that's really a challenge before I go on to something else."

"Well, you're out of luck right now," I said, "because I have to give a private lesson to a kid named Ryan in a few minutes."

A slow smile spread over his face, instantly transforming him, as it had the day before, into an almost-friendly person. "Surprise," he said, "I'm Ryan. The private lesson's with me!"

"No!"

He grinned. "I wanted to go out with you again, and I wanted to ride that big horse."

I laughed. "You think Mr. Bradley'll let you out on King?"

"Why not?" he asked coolly.

"Because he's not your average horse," I said. "You did fine yesterday on Jessie, who's very docile and obedient. King isn't like that. He's totally unpredictable. He's hardly ever been ridden, for one thing. When Mr. Bradley got him he was only half-broken, and I don't think anyone's ever going to be able to tame him. I know I'd never, ever put a new rider on his back. He'd run away with you, and you wouldn't be able to stop him."

"I'd like to try," Ryan said.

"Well, Mr. Bradley wouldn't let you," I insisted.

His steady gaze met mine. "Would *you* let me?" he asked. "We could arrange things, couldn't we? Just privately between ourselves?"

"What do you mean?"

"I mean that you go out on King and I'll ride Jessie, and when we get away from the stable, we'll swap horses."

"I can't do that! What if you fell and hurt yourself? You'd sue Mr. Bradley and I'd be out of a job."

He shook his head. "I promise I won't let you take the blame. Besides, I'm not going to fall."

There was that arrogant smile again. But

there was something else about his expression that convinced me I could trust him. "OK, I'll saddle up King."

Mr. Bradley came out to watch us leave. "Taking out King again?" he said, grinning. "Good idea. He'll be a trained horse in no time at all."

"Why does he look so pleased?" Ryan asked as we clattered out of the yard.

"Because I'm breaking this horse for him."

"So he can use him in the school?"

I let out a sharp little laugh. "No, so he can sell him for a huge profit," I grumbled.

"And do you get a cut of the profit?"

I laughed again. "That's what he promised me, but I'll be lucky if I get a thank-you."

"So why are you doing it?"

"Because I don't have a horse anymore and I need to ride," I said.

We started on the long path up the hill. King snorted steamy breath into the frosty air and danced along sideways.

Ryan moved up beside me again. "What happened?" he asked. I found the concern in his voice pleasantly surprising.

"We used to live on a ranch. My father had a heart attack and we had to move to Denver," I said.

"And you don't like it?"

"I hate it," I said. "I hate living in a poky little apartment and I'm not too crazy about my school and it breaks my heart to watch my father just sitting, not even trying to get

107

back on his feet again." The words just came spilling out and I regretted them instantly. I had no right to tell all that to a stranger, especially someone like Ryan. "I don't want to talk about it, OK?" I added.

We moved on in silence.

"Can we change horses yet?" he asked.

"I really don't want to give you King until we're clear of the street traffic," I said. "I don't want to have to come back and tell Mr. Bradley you and his precious horse are under a truck."

"I can handle that horse," he said. "I know I can."

"What makes you so confident?" I snapped. "You have the biggest swelled head I've ever seen. One of these days you're going to wake up and find something you can't do."

"Well, at least I try," he said. "I go out and do things and keep fighting. If you'd felt strongly enough about leaving your ranch and your horse, you should have fought, too."

"I did fight," I said.

"Not hard enough," he said. "You should have arranged to live with another family and keep your horse. That's what I would have done."

"Oh, sure," I snapped. "And have everyone tell me that it'd be my fault if my father had another attack worrying about me?"

"Look, his heart isn't your problem," Ryan said. "You have your own life. You have to do what you think is best for you. You can't spend your time worrying about other people."

"Are you saying that I shouldn't care that my father might die?"

He looked at me evenly. "You can care, but you can't let it wreck your life. You only have one life and you have to live it the way you want to."

King danced again, and I had to pull him up sharply. He stood there pawing at the ground. If I could have reached Ryan, I think I would have hit him.

"Boy, do you have nerve," I yelled. "What do you know about anything? A spoiled brat like you in your expensive clothes, trying riding one day and then going on to something else because riding is boring! What do you know about real life and not enough money and worrying if someone in your family is going to die?"

"I know a bit," he said quietly. "I know the only thing to do is fight."

"I said I didn't want to talk about it," I said. "Here, you can have King if you want. But I warn you, he's in a skittish mood today."

"Maybe he feels all your anger," Ryan said.

"I'm not angry!" I yelled back.

A smile crossed his face. "Then why do you keep yelling? And why don't you want to talk?"

"Did anyone ever tell you you're a very annoying person?" I said, sliding down from King's back. "I bet your girlfriend wants to scream after an hour with you. By the way,

109

dismount left side, remember? And keep hold of the reins while you walk around his head."

"Right now I don't have a girlfriend," he said. "The position is vacant—are you applying?"

"Not if you were the last boy on earth," I said.

He laughed. "That's what I thought. Here, give me King's reins."

"I'd better hold him while you get up," I said.

"It's OK. I can manage," he said, taking the reins from me.

As he put his foot into the stirrup, King immediately started waltzing. Ryan swung around for a minute, then dropped back down onto the snowy grass. I reached out and grabbed King's reins before he took off down the path. Ryan got up and brushed himself off. His face had turned bright pink again.

"OK. So hold the reins for me," he said. "And stop grinning."

"You're doing it all wrong," I said. "Watch me." I collected the reins into my left hand, slipped my left foot into the stirrup, reached for the saddle horn, and swung easily into Jessie's saddle. "Now you try," I said, holding King firmly. "And collect his reins as soon as you're in the saddle so that he can feel who's boss."

This time he mounted easily and we moved off together.

"Boy, what a difference," he said after a

while. "You can feel this horse is ready to go."

I nodded. "Just don't let him go or you won't be able to stop him."

We rode on. I had to keep urging Jessie on to keep up with King's long strides.

"Are you really a champion rider?" Ryan asked at last. "Mr. Bradley seems to think you're all set for the Olympics."

I was just about to tell him how good I was and how many trophies I had won, but I didn't. There was something about his eyes and the way he looked at me that forced me to answer modestly. "I used to think I was pretty hot stuff, back in Wyoming," I said. "But now I'm not so sure."

"Did you enter races and things?" he asked.

"Jumping mostly," I said. "English style jumping."

He looked impressed. "You mean over fences and things?"

"Fences and gates and walls. You must have seen it on TV."

His face took on a faraway look. "I'd like to try that," he said. "It must feel like flying."

"Sometimes," I said. "Most of the time all I can think about is not flying over the horse's head when he lands."

"Do you think you'll ever be a champion?"

"Hardly likely now," I said. "I don't even have a horse."

"You could train King to jump," Ryan said.

111

"I bet Mr. Bradley would love that. Good publicity for his stable!"

As he said it, I felt a lurch of fear. I could see myself on King, going over gates, feeling King's enormous power, and knowing that at any moment he might run away with me. *This is terrible*, I thought. *I can't lose my nerve just because of one stupid day.* Out loud I said, "Oh, I don't think King would make a jumper. He's too big."

Just at that moment there was a deafening noise. A giant snowplow roared its way along the road down below, then sounded a great blast on its horn. King's ears went back. "Hold on to him tightly!" I yelled.

But it was too late.

King did exactly what he had done with me. He took off like a bolt of lightning, snow and mud flying up behind him as he disappeared down the road. I urged Jessie into a gallop, but we couldn't catch them. All I could see was a golden blur ahead, receding farther and farther into the distance. Then I saw the gate across the trail ahead—a big, metal gate that was closed. Would King have the sense to stop for it as he had stopped for the tree?

King thundered toward it as I watched helplessly. Then, with one mighty spring, King was sailing over the gate, Ryan tucked in on his back. They landed on the other side and disappeared into a stand of trees. I pulled Jessie up and wondered what to do next. The gate was clearly padlocked, so I had no way of going after them. I imagined Ryan lying senseless on the trail ahead, or King writhing on the ground with a broken leg. I wondered how I was going to tell Mr. Bradley. But before I could do anything sensible about rescuing them I could feel the ground vibrating again with the thud of hooves. Ryan and King came flying back toward us, took the gate as if it were only a large stride, and pulled up beside me.

I expected Ryan to look scared and guilty. Instead his face absolutely glowed. "Did you see that?" he asked. "That was terrific! Did you see the way he jumped? He soared over it as if it was a twig. And you thought this horse wouldn't make a jumper, didn't you? And it wasn't a fluke, either. I made him do it a second time just to prove it, and he loved it. Didn't you, King?" He leaned down to pat the horse's steaming flank.

"You *made* him jump?" I stammered.

"Oh, not the first time," he admitted. "He bolted with me, just like you said he would. I was pretty scared for a moment when I saw that gate coming up. But once I got the hang of it, he stopped easily enough. In fact, he seems to understand exactly what I want him to do."

"We'd better get him home before he catches a chill," I said shakily.

"OK," Ryan agreed without an argument. "I don't want anything to happen to him now."

We walked back in silence. I sneaked a look

at him on King's back. His seat was perfect; without ever being told how to sit, he had the horse under perfect control. *He can't be a new rider*, I kept telling myself. *He can ride King the way I never could. It's just not fair.*

To stifle these mixed-up feelings I said out loud, "So now that you've tried jumping, that just about does horseback riding, unless you want to race or fly over to England and hunt."

"I've been thinking," he said seriously. "Do you think this horse would be good enough for competitions?"

"The way you sailed over that gate just then," I said, "I don't think they could build a jump high enough for him."

"So you think we could do it?" he asked.

"Do what?"

"Train King for jumping competitions. You could teach me. We could make him a proper show horse. Do you think we could?"

I looked at Ryan. His face was not the proud, cold face of the boy I had met the day before. His eyes were shining.

"Yes," I said slowly. "I really think we could."

Ryan reached out his hand to me. "Put it there, partner," he said. As his big hand closed over mine, I felt as if a powerful electric current was running all the way up my arm. I guess he must have felt it, too. For a moment we just stayed there staring at each other, our hands clasped together. Then King danced impatiently and we were drawn apart.

* * *

"So how did the private lesson go?" Mr. Bradley asked as I was unsaddling at the end of the last trail ride. "Did that boy learn a thing or two from the expert?"

"He liked it so much that he wants to take jumping lessons several times a week," I said, not looking at Mr. Bradley as I walked past him toward the tack room. I could hear his footsteps shuffling behind me, trying to keep up with my quick pace.

"Several times a week?" he roared. "He's going to pay to be here several times a week?"

"That's what it sounded like," I said. "Only we won't charge him too much, will we? Because I'm going to combine his training with breaking King, and I'm only doing that as a big favor to you."

"I'm not handing out my horses for everyone to ride free!" he grumbled, coming into the tack room behind me as I slung my saddle onto its peg.

"I didn't say free," I said calmly. "It's just that you can't afford to pay me for all the work I'm putting in on King, so you can't charge Ryan too much!"

"All right. I get the picture," he said.

"Oh, and speaking of paying," I went on, my confidence rising all the time, "you didn't pay me yet for the trail rides or the private lesson. You must have pulled in a fortune this weekend." I walked out again into the crisp night air, heading toward the feed bins.

"Yes, but what about all the weekends when

115

nobody came," Mr. Bradley insisted, following me. "I still had to feed my horses then. Hey, watch it. One scoop is enough of that stuff. Let them fill up on hay. I don't want my horses fat as pigs. I have lots of bills to catch up on, you know."

"But if you want me to lead trail rides, you're going to have to pay me."

"I wouldn't want to be your father," he muttered. "I bet you make his life miserable, bugging him all the time." He reached into his pocket and brought out an almost empty bill clip. "I don't seem to have change right now," he said. "How about next time you come?"

"I'll take a check," I said. "And I'm always very considerate to my father."

"I don't seem to have my checkbook," he said, feeling halfheartedly into his pockets.

"Sure you do. It's on the table in your office. I saw it today," I said, grinning at him.

He glared at me, but shuffled over to his office. "Did anyone ever tell you that you're bad news?" he grunted. "Do you always keep on at people until they get fed up with you and give in?"

"Most of the time," I said, watching as he scribbled a check and ripped it out.

It was only for forty dollars, which didn't include Ryan's private lesson, but somehow I sensed I'd better take what I could. I felt I had won a big victory. I had faced a mean grown-up, fought for my rights, and made him do something he hadn't wanted to. That felt pretty good. In fact, most things were beginning to feel pretty good. It would be fun to train King to be a jumper, to work with Ryan almost every day, and to have money in my pocket. For the first time since Dad's attack I had things to look forward to.

Chapter Thirteen

The next day I was hurrying home from school, moving against a stiff wind, when I saw Trisha's familiar dark hair blowing in the breeze ahead of me. As I closed in on her I noticed she was trying to balance a load of books in one arm and a violin case under the other.

"Here, let me help," I said, grabbing a couple of books. "You look like the walking Tower of Pisa."

"Oh, thanks, Eden," she said breathlessly. "I *am* a walking disaster area. Why did my English teacher have to give an essay assignment the same night I planned to write my government term paper! And a violin recital on top of everything!"

I was sorry to hear about her heavy workload but glad I was able to help her out. I could remember all too clearly how I had snubbed all her attempts to help me.

"So what have you been doing the past week? I hardly ever see you around anymore," Trisha said.

"I've found something to do with myself at last. I'm working at a stable," I said.

"You got a job?" she asked, pushing the heavy front door open and stepping ahead of me into the blissful warmth of the front hall.

"Yeah, I'm training a horse and giving private lessons to a boy."

"Ah-ha," she said, punching at the elevator button with a finger she managed to get free. A slow smile spread over her face. "Now I get it. A boy, huh. I thought you looked different. Your face looks more alive."

"That's the wind," I said too rapidly. "Not any boy."

"Sure," she said, nodding wisely. She stepped out of the elevator ahead of me on the fourth floor. "Want to come in for a while? I baked some terrific chocolate-chip cookies yesterday. There should be some left, if the vultures in my family haven't eaten them all."

I was about to refuse because I had to get down to the stables. Then I realized she was trying to be friendly, and that it would look like I was snubbing her yet again. Even a nice person like Trisha wouldn't keep trying to make friends forever, and even I, dumb and stubborn as I was, was beginning to realize that life without friends could be pretty miserable. "Thanks," I said, "but I can only stay a few minutes. I can't keep the boss waiting."

"Or the boy?" Trisha asked, ushering me into a warm, comfortable living room. I was immediately struck by the difference between this and our rooms down the hall. The rooms were exactly the same size, but Trisha's looked like a home. Her parents had made their rooms look pretty and comfortable and lived-in—as if they intended to stay there forever and ever. Our living room looked like a place to store furniture until we found somewhere better. Surely my parents couldn't enjoy living in a bleak and poky little apartment that wasn't a home.

But Mom hadn't had the time to fix up our place, and Dad hadn't had the energy. I realized then that I had to do my share. I'd try to put some time into our home. We couldn't keep hoping to move into the dream apartment we might never own.

"Your living room looks so pretty," I said.

Trisha looked around and nodded. "I like it," she said. "It's a bit untidy for some people, but I like that, too. Living in one of those showplace houses would make me nervous. Would you like a soda with your cookies or a glass of milk?"

"Soda would be fine," I said, putting down her pile of books on a maple coffee table and sinking back into the pillows on the print sofa. Trish came back in with a tray as I was halfway through examining a whole bank of family photographs.

"Don't look at the one of me when I was seven," she warned. "I was a horrible little blimp. Here, try the cookies while they're hot. I put them in the microwave for a few seconds."

The warm chocolate spread deliciously through my mouth. "These are great," I said, finishing the rest rapidly. "You've got to teach me how to make them if you ever have time."

"They're easy," she said. "Come on over anytime and I'll show you." She picked up her glass of soda and took a sip. "Have you decided to give up on the boy back in Wyoming?" she asked.

"Because of this boy I'm riding with?" I asked cautiously. "Oh, no," I said, hedging. Even though I'd realized in my heart that Ted and I were through I clung to the illusion he was still waiting for me—at least as far as others were concerned. It was hard to admit I'd been dumped, even if Ted had tried to do it in a nice way.

"But it can't do any harm to make some friends closer to home!"

I shook my head very firmly. "No, thank you," I said. "I don't see this guy I give lessons to as a future boyfriend. To be honest with you, he's a bit of a pain. Talk about conceited! He thinks he knows everything and can do everything." I sighed. "The trouble is—he can."

"What's his name? Is he from around here?"

"Ryan Benson," I said. "And I don't know where he's from."

Trisha furrowed her brow. "Very tall with blond hair?" she asked.

"Yeah, do you know him?"

"He used to go to our school," Trisha said. "He left last summer to go to some private school, I think."

"I don't know," I said. "We've only known each other a couple of days, and we don't talk much about our personal lives. I don't want to and I guess he doesn't, either. All I know is that he used to be a great skier and he doesn't have a girlfriend."

"What do you mean *used* to be a great skier? He was president of the ski club here."

"He told me he'd quit skiing," I said. "I don't know why. But I get the impression that as soon as he can do something, he gets bored with it and drops it."

"That's funny," Trisha said, frowning as if she were trying to remember something. "That doesn't sound like Ryan. Of course, I never really knew him."

"I don't really want to know more about him," I said. "He's not the sort of person I'd want to become involved with. All I want to do is teach him how to take a horse over jumps and then go home and forget about him."

"OK. I get the message," Trisha said, grinning at me. "Although he sure is cute."

"Very cute," I said. "But that still doesn't mean that I'm about to fall in love with him."

"Guess what," I called to Ryan as I saddled up King that afternoon. "I've found out about your murky past."

I'd expected him to grin or say something rude to me. Instead he went deathly white. "You've found out what?" he asked.

"Boy, what are you so guilty about?" I said. "All I meant was that I just found out you used to go to my school. Isn't that a coincidence?"

"Who was talking about me? What did you tell them?" Ryan demanded.

"What could I tell them? I don't know anything about you—except that you're not the easiest person in the world to teach!'"

I turned away from him. He came over and put a hand gently on my shoulder. "Believe me, it's better for both of us if you don't know anything about me," he said quietly. "Please don't tell anyone else you know me. Promise."

"I promise."

Of course I wondered what he must have to hide. Surely if there had been some scandal when he left, everyone would have heard about it. You can't keep juicy gossip secret in high schools! So the next day I asked Renee if she knew Ryan, pretending I had found an old homework paper of his stuck in one of my books. She told me he'd been a very cute and very popular junior who'd left school the year before. She hadn't known why and was curious to know what had become of him. It took all my willpower to keep my mouth shut, but I wanted to keep my promise to Ryan.

So I was no closer to solving Ryan's mysterious behavior, but if nothing else, meeting Ryan had helped take me out of my shell. The more I was with him, the more mysterious he became, and the more determined I became to break through his defenses. But even though he was no longer rude or defensive to me, he deliberately continued to shut me out of the rest of his life.

One day in early March he followed me into the tack room when I went to get King's evening feed. He was feeling very giddy, having managed to get King through a double jump, something King hated to do.

"So, do you reckon we'll win at the State Fair?" he asked, standing behind me as I dipped into the big barrel with the scoop.

"Hey, steady there," I said, not turning around. "You've only just managed a double. The triple's still waiting, and the water jump, and then putting it all together into a big long course."

"No problem," he said smoothly. "I can see it all now—leading King around with his blue ribbon on, accepting all the compliments, considering whether to join the Olympic team."

I turned around and saw that he was teasing me. His blue eyes were sparkling, holding mine.

"Boy, you don't suffer from lack of ambition, do you?" I asked, laughing.

"No," he said, making a face at me.

"Oh, shut up," I said, flicking a handful of bran playfully up into his face.

Ryan shook his head wildly and grabbed at my wrists. "Hey, you're dangerous," he said.

Suddenly I was very conscious of his holding me very close, his hands tight around my wrists, his face only inches from mine. "You're making me spill the bran," I said weakly, not knowing whether I wanted to encourage him or not.

His eyes still challenged mine. "Didn't anyone ever tell you that throwing bran in a guy's face is an old-fashioned method of flirtation?" he asked, grinning down at me.

I shook my head. He released my wrists.

"You're spilling the bran," he said. "Mr. Bradley will be mad at you." Then he dodged out of the room, leaving me wondering whether I was glad he had gone or not.

But as the days went by, I was no nearer to finding out anything. Ryan laughed with me, teased me sometimes, lost his temper with me a few times, but still kept me at a distance. I began to feel really confused: we were sharing so much, working with King every day. Why did he always shut me out at the last minute? And why was that bothering me more and more with each passing day?

There were times when he really stretched my emotions to the breaking point. One day King refused to change feet before a big jump and skidded to a halt, tossing me over the jump without him. I lay there with all the air knocked out of me, wondering if I had broken anything. When Ryan appeared, all he did was stand there laughing. That made me so mad I sat up.

"So that's the way you get him to change feet?" he asked. "Very interesting. But I always thought you were supposed to take the horse over the jumps with you."

"Very funny, Mr. Wise Guy," I snapped, struggling to my feet. "Did it occur to you that I might have broken something? I don't believe you care about anyone or anything in this whole world except your own precious self! Well, since you already know it all, you train King. I'll go on home." I stalked away.

Ryan leaped after me and grabbed my arm. "No, Eden, don't go. I'm sorry," he said plaintively. "I do need you. I keep trying to tell myself that I don't need anybody, but I guess I do."

"You sure don't act like it," I said, turning away from him, confused by his strong grip on my arm. "I thought we were getting to be friends."

"I want to be friends," he said. "It's just

that I can't really be friends with anyone right now."

"Why not?" I asked. "Why do you always have to be so secretive? If you have a problem, you can tell me, you know."

He let go of my arm abruptly. "That's just it," he said. "I can't tell you. I can't tell anyone." He turned away, his attention now on King. "I'd better see if I can make him change feet before that wall."

I ran after him. "Why, Ryan?" I pleaded. "Why are you shutting me out of your life?"

He wouldn't answer. The cold stare he flashed at me indicated clearly that the conversation was finished.

Somehow I managed to get through the rest of the lesson, despite the tears that threatened to betray my true feelings. Though I tried to hide it from myself, now there was no denying the truth—I was starting to care for Ryan Benson very much.

Chapter Fourteen

"So how are things down at the manure pile?" Renee asked as I passed her in the hall one afternoon that week. "Are you still going down there every day?"

"That's right," I said, grinning. "Every day and loving it."

She shook her head in disbelief. "Will you be back in time for the basketball game tonight?"

"I don't know," I said hesitantly.

"Oh, you should come," Renee insisted. "I'll save you a seat if you like."

"Thanks," I said. "If I get back early enough I'll come."

On the way home I decided that I had come a long way in the past few weeks. I didn't mind if Renee teased me anymore. Everyone in her group used put-downs in normal conversation, and I was getting pretty good at it myself. Also I could look forward to things like basketball games again. I really was beginning to live.

I wished I could have said the same about my father. His initial enthusiasm about the hardware store had died down, and he was now using Denver's cold winter weather as an excuse not to go out and check on the store's renovation. If only I could get *him* interested in life again, I thought.

I rushed home, hung up my good clothes, and wriggled into my old jeans. I was just about to go out again when I saw my father sleeping in his armchair. His mouth was open and his flesh seemed to have shrunk so that his face looked like a skull. He was so still that I had a sudden fear he might be dead. I crept over to him, put my face close to his, and felt a small puff of breath on my cheek. I was just straightening up again when he opened his eyes.

"Why, Eden, you startled me," he said. "I didn't even hear you come in."

"Are you OK?" I asked. "You were lying there so still."

"Just had a little nap," he said.

"Did you go over to the store today?" I asked.

"I was going to, but I didn't get around to it."

"Oh, Dad." I sighed. "The store will never get finished at this rate."

He looked at me calmly. "New catalog came from that tool company in Chicago. I had to study that awhile."

"But, Dad, what good is it to talk about buying tools when the store isn't even ready? Those carpenters you hired don't do a thing unless you go down there and make them work."

"All in good time, Eden," my father said. "We can't rush things. That's what my doctor told me."

I turned away. "I've got to go," I said. "Ryan will be waiting and he gets mad if I'm late."

"How is that going?" my father asked—out of politeness, I felt.

"Fine. You should see that horse jump! If we can only get him to obey signals a bit quicker, he'll be ready for some shows this spring."

"That's good," my father said, sitting back and closing his eyes.

"Why don't you come down sometime and check him out? It would do you good to watch King jump."

A tired smile passed over his face. "Maybe I will," he said. "When it's a bit warmer out."

"The weather's not bad," I said encouragingly. "In fact, it's beautiful out today. The snow's all gone and the sun's out."

There was a faint light in his eyes. "Does the wind smell of spring yet? Do you remember how we could always smell the spring back home? Everything smelled green. Is it like that?"

"Why don't you come out and see for yourself?"

"You know I can't, Eden."

"You could if you tried, Dad. You could if you really wanted to. But I don't think you want to," I blurted out.

"Of course I do," he said. But I sensed defeat in his voice.

"Then why don't you start making an effort?" I pressed on, determined to get him going again. "Why don't you go down to the store? Why don't you start taking walks?"

"Because I'm not allowed to yet, that's why." He was sitting up now, almost yelling. "Everyone tells me to take it easy, not to rush things."

"Not everyone. I'm telling you to get out there. Get going again!"

"But you don't really understand, Eden."

"I understand that you're my dad, and I love you, and I hate seeing you like this!" I said angrily. "Sometimes I think you're afraid to get better!"

I snatched up my jacket and ran out before I said anything more.

When I got to the stables, Ryan was inside the field leaning back against the fence, staring out in front of him. King was munching at a tuft of grass beside him. I couldn't help but notice how good they looked together;

131

Ryan's blond hair blended perfectly with King's coat. That day Ryan was wearing a long-sleeved T-shirt, and his body had the same sleek, powerful elegance about it that King's had. I stood staring at them for a while, feeling a sort of tender pride in them, as if they were both my creations.

Finally I walked up to them. At the sound of my footsteps, they both looked up. "Oh, there you are at last," Ryan said. "We're both freezing to death. What took you so long?"

The bubble of tender pride popped instantly. "That's what I call a real warm greeting," I said sarcastically.

"Hey, what's eating you?" he asked.

"Oh, nothing," I said. "I had a fight with my father."

Ryan's eyes opened wide. "And you're taking it out on me?"

"I am not! You're the one with the chip on your shoulder." I slammed the gate shut behind me. King threw up his head in alarm and galloped off across the field.

"Now look what you've done," I said, starting after him. "You'd better catch him before he puts a foot through his reins and breaks a leg."

"*I've* done?" Ryan demanded, running after me. "I like that. You were the one who was yelling and thumping."

"But you started it."

"Do you always blame other people for everything that goes wrong in your life?" he shouted. We closed in on King, who eyed us suspiciously and danced away at the last moment.

"Well, I don't seem to have much control over the things that go wrong," I yelled. "Here, grab him, quick!"

As I made a lunge at King's bridle, Ryan went for the other side of his head and missed. King speeded up again and I went sprawling onto the wet, cold grass. I hadn't worn a parka that day, and I could feel the wetness seeping in through my sweater and jeans. *OK*, I said to myself, lying there, not moving. *Every time I can't believe another thing can go wrong, it does. Well, I give up. I'm not going to fight it anymore.*

Then I felt Ryan's hand on my back. "Eden?" he asked. "Are you OK?"

I turned my head to look at him. "Oh, I'm fine," I said. "Lying in cold water is very healthy, they say. In fact I'm having such a good time I've officially decided to call it tomorrow. Today no longer exists."

He gave a little laugh. "Here, come on, you'll catch pneumonia," he said. He reached out his hand to me and pulled me to my feet. "We all have bad days, and this is just one of yours."

"I know," I said, brushing off the mud and grass. "The only trouble is that I can't remember what the good days were like."

"Hey, it's not as bad as that," Ryan said. "We had a good day last Sunday when we got

King to go over the wall. I felt great when I got home, like I could do anything. Didn't you feel like that?"

"Yes," I said quietly. "Yes, I did."

"Come on," he said. He wrapped his arms around me in a bear hug. "Everything will be just fine," he said. "Everything's *got* to be just fine."

His tenderness was more upsetting than his insults or teasing. I could feel something snap inside me. The hopelessness of my father constantly sitting in his chair, of the hardware store which would never be finished, and of the boy who kept pushing me away overwhelmed me. "No, it won't be fine," I said, as tears welled up in my eyes. "I don't know how to cope with my father and I don't know how to cope with you." I started to cry shamelessly.

Ryan continued to hold me silently. I could feel the warmth of his shoulder through his T-shirt.

"It's no use, Eden," he whispered. "I can't go on like this, either. It's eating me up as well. I'm really the sort of person who cares a lot. But lately I've been trying really hard to stop feeling anything."

"But why, Ryan?" I asked. It came out as a sort of hiccup. "Why would you want to do that?"

"I have my reasons," he said.

"There you go again," I pleaded. "You always shut me out. Don't you see how that hurts me?"

Ryan reached out his hand and stroked a tear from my cheek. "Eden," he said in a choked voice, "it's only because I care about you that I've been trying to keep you away. I didn't want you to get involved with me, and I didn't want to get involved with you, either. But I guess I am. I can't help what I feel about you—and it's all so hopeless."

I looked up and saw the bleak despair in his eyes. "Ryan, what is it?" I asked. "Are you in some kind of trouble?"

"Big trouble," he said, "but not the way you think." He sighed deeply. "I wasn't going to tell anybody this, ever," he said. "I even changed schools so I wouldn't have to face anybody I knew. But I owe you an explanation—if only so you won't hate me."

"I couldn't hate you," I said. "I've tried and it's no good!"

He smiled again. "I can imagine," he said. "I've heard myself being rude, and it's like I'm outside, watching another person. I thought I could keep other people away from me. I didn't want anyone close to me because I couldn't stand their pity."

"Pity about what?"

"I found out awhile ago that I have MS," he said. He must have noticed my blank look. "Multiple sclerosis, you know what that means?" he asked.

"Only that it's some sort of disease."

"There's no cure," he said bleakly. "Eventually I'll get weaker and weaker until all my muscles stop working. I'll probably end up in a wheelchair."

"But you're so strong!" I blurted out before I could stop myself. "Look how you control that horse. They must have gotten it wrong."

"No, they didn't get it wrong," he said, shaking his head. "I had one bad attack last spring. I fell when I was skiing and my legs wouldn't obey me. They did all these tests. I thought I'd just had a fall. I wouldn't admit to myself that I'd lost control of my legs."

"Ryan, how terrible," I said. "But your legs are fine now, aren't they?"

He scowled as he stared out past me across the field. The light was fading and there was a thin band of red behind the western hills. The trees stood out in a delicate tracery of black. "That's just the problem," he said bitterly. "With this disease you never know which muscle is going to go and when. A couple of times my face muscles wouldn't behave properly, and I sounded weird when I talked. I'm supposed to be taking it easy. In fact, my mother would have a fit if she knew what I was doing with King. She thinks I'm trotting along on trail rides. I'm not supposed to take any chances, you see. But I'm the sort of person who likes to take chances. I decided I had to try everything once, just to know what it felt like. I didn't mean to get stuck on one thing at all. . . ." His voice trailed away as he gazed down at me. "And I didn't intend to feel anything for anybody ever again. Especially not somebody like you who has enough problems of her own. But I do, Eden. I think I'm falling in love with you. Dumb, isn't it?"

"I don't think it's dumb at all," I whispered.

"You understand now, don't you?" he asked. "I don't want you to get involved with a hopeless person like me."

"I already *am* involved," I said. "And you're not a hopeless person. You told me I had to fight and not give up. I think you're right. And maybe it's easier to fight when there are two of you."

"Oh, Eden," he whispered. His arms came around me. His lips were searching frantically for mine. Ted's kisses had made me feel wonderful, but they were nothing like Ryan's. I felt as if a powerful electric shock were rushing through my body so that I was tingling all over. I wasn't even conscious of the cold wind blowing down from the hills or my slightly damp clothes. Nothing mattered except Ryan's strong arms around me and his lips crushed against mine.

King was the one who brought us down to earth again. Obviously he'd gotten tired of standing there when he could be back in his stable with his feed in front of him. He walked up to us silently, and suddenly we were conscious of his hot breath on our necks. We broke apart.

"OK, we get the hint," Ryan said. "I'm not

137

going to bring you along next time. You're a real party pooper." King tossed his head as if he understood, and we both laughed.

"You should thank him for bringing us together," I said. "If you hadn't seen him at the stable you'd be racing motorcycles by now."

"Maybe that would have been better for both of us," Ryan said.

"Oh, come on. No more of that," I said firmly. "From now on I forbid any gloomy thoughts. We're going to enter this horse in a show, and you're going to win a blue ribbon. Do you understand me?"

"Yes, ma'am," he said, grinning. His face suddenly looked young and boyish and relaxed —as if someone had finally removed a terrible load from his shoulders. "Come on, let's get this horse back to his stable. I don't think any of us feels like working today. Then I'll drive you home."

Chapter Fifteen

It was just getting to be dark when we pulled up outside my apartment house. We hadn't talked much on the ride home, but we sat so close we were touching. Words didn't seem so important now.

"Er, are you sure you wouldn't like to come up for a while and meet my folks?" I asked haltingly.

He grinned that wonderful boyish, teasing grin. "No, thanks," he said quickly. Then he reached over and touched my arm. "Hey, don't get me wrong," he said. "I'm not shutting you out again. It's just that—oh, it's hard to explain. Look, Eden, do you really have to go home now? I mean, could we go for a drive first? Just somewhere to talk? I've shut up like a clam for so long that just talking would feel good."

"Fine with me," I said. "But I'd really better run up and tell my folks, or they'll worry about me."

"You have that problem, too?"

I sighed. "It comes with being an only child."

"Same with me," Ryan said.

"I'll be right back," I said, bounding away from him into the building. When I got upstairs, I poked my head around the door and saw my mother. "Don't wait supper for me, I'm going out with a friend for a while," I yelled. Then I ran down the stairs.

"Boy, that was quick," Ryan said, looking impressed when I returned.

I smiled. "I didn't give them time to answer," I said.

He started the engine again and the little sports car shot forward.

"Don't they have a speed limit in this city?" I asked after a while.

Ryan laughed. "Come on, it feels so good. I have a motorbike, but they won't let me ride that anymore. I used to love to ride it because you get this incredible feeling of speed on a bike that you never get in a car!"

"I'm getting a feeling of speed right now," I said, giving him a sideways glance. "And I'm also getting a feeling we'll be seeing a flashing light in the rearview mirror any moment."

"All right," Ryan said. "I'll slow down." He

slipped an arm around my shoulder. "You're a slave driver, did anyone ever tell you that?"

"Never," I said, snuggling up to him. "Everyone else thinks I'm a quiet, shy little thing."

"I don't believe that for a minute," he said. "Don't you yell at the rest of your friends the way you yell at me on that horse?"

"I haven't made a lot of real friends here yet," I said after a while.

"How come?"

"I felt out of place when I moved here, so I shut myself off from other people. They all seemed to live in a different world from me. You're the only person I've met who's on my wavelength."

"What about back in wherever-it-was?" Ryan asked. "Didn't you have friends there?"

"Lots," I said. "But that's different. I was born there. They were all kids like me. Nobody there thought you were weird if you hadn't seen the latest movie, because the latest movie didn't get to us for a couple of months."

Ryan turned off the busy street and drove into a darkened park near the state capitol. Water from a lake reflected the building lights.

"What about a boyfriend?" Ryan asked. "Did you have one back there?"

"Yes, I did."

Silence.

"And do you still think about him?"

Another long pause.

"Sometimes."

141

"Is it all over between you?"

"Yes," I answered quietly.

"Was that tough on you?"

I nodded. "Ted was really nice. He was friendly, and he laughed a lot. And he was really popular at school, and a super jock."

"Exactly the opposite from me," Ryan said sharply. He screeched to a halt in the deserted park. On the other side of the lake we could see the red taillights and white headlights of homebound commuters, but there we were in a pool of blackness. Ryan turned to me again. "Look, Eden," he said. "I don't want you hanging around because you feel sorry for me! I don't want anyone's pity!"

I could barely see his face in the darkened car, but I could see his eyes—frightened, hopeful, hopeless, little boy's eyes—watching me and pleading with me. I leaned across and kissed him on the lips, gently at first, then not so gently. "Does that feel like pity?" I murmured. I heard him give a little sigh of content before I was enveloped in a bear hug and he was kissing me again.

"Hey, Ryan," I said when I could finally speak. "I thought you asked me to come for a drive and talk! You lured me here under false pretenses!"

"You started it," Ryan said, his eyes teasing mine. "You were doing the luring."

"You told me I was a bossy slave driver," I said, snuggling against his chest.

His arms tightened around me. "I want you

142

to be strong," he said. "I need you to be strong, because sometimes I'm scared that I won't be strong enough."

"I'm not very strong," I said. "I cracked under all that pressure of moving. But I'll be around whenever you need me, Ryan."

"I can't believe I was lucky enough to have found you," he said, kissing my forehead lightly. "I couldn't face the kids at Evans— they all thought I was a real Mr. Macho. Now I go to a snobby private school, and the other kids think I'm the snobbiest of all because I stay away from everyone."

"But why didn't you come right out and tell your friends?" I asked. "I'm sure they would have understood if they were real friends."

"Because I'm too proud, I guess," he said. "Dumb, I know, but I couldn't imagine showing up there in a wheelchair one day and having everyone hovering around me saying 'Poor Ryan. Isn't it terrible. Do you remember when he used to be a ski champ?'"

"I understand," I said. "I'd feel the same way myself."

"That's what made me notice you," Ryan said. "You were so feisty and rude to me. I thought that you were someone who wouldn't fuss over me."

"Does your mother pamper you?"

He laughed. "You'd better believe it. If I sneeze, she's on the phone with my doctor. If I reach for the peanut butter jar by myself, she leaps up to do it for me! I can hardly stand to be in the house."

"What about your father? Is he the same?"

There was a cold silence. Then he said, "My father lives in New York. He's made a lot of money and he supports us well, but he never comes to visit. He's too busy doing his own thing. He told my mother that they married too young, and she tied him down. I guess she did. I guess we both did—but I'd never go off and leave my family because they tied me down."

I could hear the bitterness in his voice. "I know just how you feel," I said. "It's hard when parents act as if you don't even exist."

Ryan took my hand and held it tightly. "It's scary how much we have in common," he said. "We can understand each other because we've both been through the same things. It's almost as if we were meant to meet, as if fate had everything planned. We're both at new schools and we haven't made close friends at them yet. We both have problems with our families. I think that's why I didn't want to come up and meet yours. I want to keep us as our own little secret. Do you know what I mean?"

"I think so," I said hesitantly. I wasn't so sure it was a good idea, but I didn't want to say the wrong thing to Ryan right then.

"I just can't be around people who'd ask me dumb questions or feel sorry for me," he said. "I don't want their pity."

"I don't think the kids at school would pity you, Ryan," I began.

Ryan interrupted me firmly. "I don't want anything to spoil the way things are between you and me."

"Don't worry," I said, "I don't want anything to spoil things, either. You're the first good thing that's happened to me in a long while."

"I wouldn't call me a good thing," he said.

"Didn't I forbid all gloomy thoughts today?" I said, grabbing his hands.

"You *are* a slave driver," he said, grinning. "But don't change. I like you the way you are."

Chapter Sixteen

I had no idea what time I let myself into our apartment, but both my parents were up waiting for me, facing the door with worried expressions on their faces.

"Eden, where have you been?" my mother demanded.

I looked from one face to the other. "I told you to go ahead and have supper without me," I said.

"But it's nearly midnight, Eden," my father said. "We were worried silly."

"I was out with a friend," I said. "We were just driving around and talking and we stopped for a pizza."

"You should have called. We didn't know where you could have been for so long."

146

"You know about Ryan," I said. "I've told you lots about him."

"You mean the boy down at the stables?" my father asked in amazement. "I thought you said he was a big pain."

I couldn't stop a huge grin from spreading across my face.

"Well, Jake, I don't think she feels he's a big pain anymore," my mother said, smiling.

"So when are you going to bring him around to meet us, Eden?" my father asked.

"I don't know," I said. "He's kind of shy about meeting new people."

"Well, Eden," my mother said firmly. "Back in Wyoming we would never have let you go out with a boy we hadn't met. We still feel the same way."

"He's a perfectly nice, normal boy, Mom," I explained.

"I'd still like to meet him, Eden," my father insisted. "It would make me feel more comfortable if you're going to be out driving with him until all hours."

"I'll ask him," I said hesitantly.

"This Ryan," my father said, sitting forward in his chair. "He's the one who's training the new horse for trials, isn't he?"

"That's right," I said.

I told Ryan the next day, "My parents want to meet you."

Ryan wrinkled his nose. "I didn't want you to tell them about me, remember?" he asked.

"How could I not tell them?" I asked, grinning. "They took one look at my face and they knew something special had happened."

"Did you tell them about my illness?"

"Of course not. I'm not stupid. Do you think the best way to create a good first impression would be to say, 'By the way, this boy has a terribly quick temper, drives too fast, and has an incurable disease. Apart from that he's fine'? I told them you were a nice, normal boy and they'd enjoy meeting you."

"Boy, you're a real smooth liar."

"I am not," I said hotly. "You'd be a nice, normal boy if you'd get that chip off your shoulder. And you should start mixing with people again. When I first came here I shut myself off from everybody. I thought I didn't want friends, but I was wrong. Everybody needs people to care about them. I'm getting on much better with the girls at school now, and I don't dread going there anymore."

Ryan frowned, looking for a moment as hostile and withdrawn as he had when I first met him. "Yes, well, there were nicer kids at Evans. My new school is full of snobs."

"That's what I thought about Evans," I said. "Like when the girls talked about skiing at Aspen and all the latest movies I hadn't seen. I thought they were deliberately making me look small. Of course, they weren't at all. The skiing and the movies were part of their normal lives, and I had to learn to fit in with them. I bet you could make friends at your new school."

"I don't want friends," Ryan said. "I don't want anybody—except maybe you." He looked at me softly, all the tension melting from his face as he smiled at me.

"Then I'm afraid you'll have to come and meet my family," I said, reaching out to stroke his hand. "We come as a group package."

"Eden, I really don't want—" he began, but I cut him off.

"I'm asking you, Ryan," I said. "If you really care about me."

He covered my hand with his own. "I guess I'd do anything for you," he said. "But don't you dare tell them about me."

Actually I needn't have worried. Their first meeting went smoothly. My mother took one look at Ryan's thin face and immediately rushed out to the kitchen to start cooking something. My father made polite conversation about horses, and before I could carry in the tray of drinks and cookies, they were into a big discussion about what horses really see when they race toward obstacles. In the end I had to drag Ryan away.

"Neat guy, your dad," he said as we climbed into his car.

"You did him a lot of good," I said, snuggling up to him. "It's the first time he's wanted to talk about anything other than what his doctor said and what medications he's taking."

"Maybe I'd better stop by more often," Ryan said. "Just to see your dad, that is. Not that I'd want to see more of you!"

He dodged as I aimed a playful punch at his arm.

But however much Ryan had enjoyed meeting my folks, he was still determined that nobody at his old school know about him. "Just think how you'd feel," he told me just before he drove me home, "if you went back to your school in Wyoming and the kids knew you were really ill. They'd either be embarrassed or make a horrible fuss over you. Either way it would be bad news. Let me just keep the good memories I've got!"

But it was hard to keep a secret. During that next week at school I had to invent letters and phone calls from Ted to explain the dreamy look that came into my eyes every time I thought about Ryan. And that was pretty often! I thought about him all day and every day. I even got into trouble for gazing out of the window during math class, and I'd always been a model student!

Ted had been a good boyfriend. He was a lot of fun and kind and popular. But ours was a superficial relationship and, even though I never admitted it, I was always on guard with him. With Ryan, though, I never had to think first about saying the right thing. We didn't even have to talk. We could sit together in the car in a wonderful, comfortable silence, almost as if we could read each other's thoughts.

One day when I was traveling to the stables on the bus, I thought to myself, *You should be feeling really depressed right now. You've met the right boy and you've fallen in love and you have nothing but heartbreak ahead of you.* But I couldn't feel like that. It was as if a big spring of happiness was bubbling up inside me, as if I had just woken up and every morning was Christmas.

I think Ryan felt the same. That proud, suspicious look had gone from his face and he laughed a lot.

Even Mr. Bradley noticed it immediately.

"All right," he growled one day when I was rubbing down the horses. "What's with you and that boy?"

"What do you mean?" I asked, feeling my cheeks turning pink. I was grateful that the light in the stall was so bad.

"He used to walk around ready to bite off my head," Mr. Bradley said. "Now he's got this silly grin on his face all the time." He paused and looked at me. "I'll have some money for you, end of today," he said shortly. "Reckon you're doing a good job with that horse. Reckon the boy thinks so, too!" Then he stomped off before I could answer.

I think King could also sense the positive energy flowing when Ryan and I were around. He suddenly became much less difficult to train, almost as if he wanted to please us.

We had set that coming Friday, the second one in March, as the deadline to take King through the whole course without stopping. So far we had only worked him through one or two jumps at a time. The double and triple jumps were the ones that gave both Ryan and King trouble. Ryan didn't yet have the experience to keep King's stride small enough between the obstacles and King was convinced he could sail over the whole combination at once if anyone would let him.

On Friday I set up a course with a triple in it, just to see what happened. King jumped the brushwood fences at the beginning as if they were nothing. Ryan swung him around hard and made him change lead feet. King went over the uneven gate with a foot to spare. He loved the white gate, so he soared over that, his tail streaming out behind him like a flash of silver fire. Then came the triple. This time Ryan had control of him, made him take one step between the first two parts and two small steps in the second. Last came the big wall, put there deliberately after the triple because you needed a giant stride and lots of speed to get over it. King cleared it easily, and Ryan brought him over to me, his face glowing with delight.

"Did you see that!" he yelled, sliding from King's back. "He did everything I told him. He jumped everything!"

"Only because you gave him the right commands," I yelled back, running toward him.

Ryan opened his arms, scooped me up, and twirled me around delightedly. I could feel his heart beating furiously against mine.

"No, Eden, it was you," he said, lowering me gently to the ground, holding me tightly in his arms. "When we win the world championship I'm going to tell the international press, 'She's the one who taught me everything I know!' "

His eyes gazed down into mine. His lips were inches away. "You'll say that?" I whispered.

"I'll say more than that," he whispered back. "I'll tell them that you gave me something to live for again."

Chapter Seventeen

From that day on we spent every spare moment together. We went bowling and ice-skating. We drove go-carts and played miniature golf. Everything Ryan did, he did well. He bowled strikes and whizzed around the middle of the ice rink. He drove his go-cart as if he were racing in the Indy Five Hundred. It was as if he was constantly saying to himself, "I can still do this. There is still time to hope."

One day we dared each other to walk across the ice on the ornamental pond near Red Rocks Park. The water below wasn't deep, but it was very cold and the ice was just ready to break up. I went first, listening to it creak protestingly. I was almost at the other side when Ryan came after me.

"Get back, you idiot!" I yelled. "It won't hold both of us!"

"Last one across is a rotten egg!" he yelled, laughing wildly as he sprinted past me.

There was a loud groan from the ice. We both leaped for the shore. The last block broke away and tipped so that we slithered into a foot of cold water.

We were just clambering out when a park attendant ran up and yelled at us, waving a stick. We took one look, Ryan grabbed my hand, and we tore off across the grass, giggling like kindergarteners.

One evening in late March we went to a carnival that had come to a shopping center on the edge of town. Bravely I followed Ryan onto everything and clutched his hand while we were whirled and tossed and dropped from great heights.

"That was fun, wasn't it?" Ryan said as we drove home afterward.

"Oh, sure," I said dryly. "I haven't had so much fun since my last visit to the dentist."

He looked at me, surprised. "Didn't you enjoy it? You weren't screaming or anything."

"That was because my jaw muscles were frozen from terror," I said.

"But why didn't you say so, Eden?" Ryan asked.

"Because you were having such a great time. I didn't want to spoil it for you."

"Such devotion," he said teasingly.

"But don't ask me to go there again," I

said. "My knees are still like jelly. And much as I love you, I don't think I could face the scream machine again in a hurry."

Ryan brought the car to a halt, right in the middle of nowhere.

"Do you?" he asked, peering at me seriously through the darkness.

"Do I what?" I asked, puzzled.

"You said that you loved me. Did you mean it?" he asked.

"Yes," I said haltingly. "I do love you."

"I love you, too, Eden," he said in a choked voice. "I've never said that to any girl before. I've always had lots of girlfriends but I've never, ever really been in love. It's a scary feeling, isn't it?"

"Scary and wonderful at the same time," I said.

Ryan stared ahead of him into the night. Then he said quietly, "I'm glad I've got you, Eden. There might not be any more carnivals."

"Nonsense," I said brightly, even though I felt the cold touch of fear spreading through me. "You're fine. Maybe those dumb old doctors were wrong. Maybe nothing will happen for years."

"I just keep thinking everything is too good to last," he said. "Now that I've found you, everything makes sense again. I keep worrying in case I wake up one morning and find that you've just melted away."

I touched his hand. "Don't worry," I said.

"I'm not going to melt away. I'm not Frosty the Snowman, you know."

"I guessed that," he said, a mischievous smile flashing across his face. And we spent the next few minutes not thinking about anything at all.

As we got to know each other better, we spent less and less time on actual "dates." We were content to do nothing except be together. We would walk, side by side, through Sloan Lake Park, talking about everything from our earliest childhoods to whether people would ever live on Mars. Sometimes we didn't talk at all. I would walk beside Ryan, feeling his hand, strong and warm, encircling mine. Every now and then we would turn and look at each other, both of us wanting to make sure that the other was really there.

One Sunday in early April Ryan and I took a picnic up into the hills toward Rocky Mountain National Park. We drove until the last straggling suburbs of the city were left behind. Fields of new wheat and alfalfa spread out as bright green carpets on either side. Fruit trees were heavy with blossoms. Birds darted ahead of us. We passed lonely farmhouses with sagging red barns and horses in fields. Some were dairy farms, some cattle ranches. I stared at them as they flashed past, trying to remember the time when I took it for granted that everyone lived like that.

"Do you miss the country?" Ryan asked,

making me wonder once again if he could actually read my thoughts.

"I miss all that space around me," I said. "At first I thought I'd never get used to being crowded with all those other people and all that noise. But now I don't even wake up at night when the fire trucks go past."

"I suppose you can get used to anything in the end," Ryan said. "Sometimes I wonder, though."

I knew what he was wondering. He was wondering if he would ever get used to the possibility of spending the rest of his life in a wheelchair.

"Oh, look at the baby calves," I said. "They can't be more than a few days old."

"They look so fragile with their spindly little legs," Ryan said, "like something out of a Walt Disney movie."

I laughed. "You try lifting a few onto the back of a truck and you'll see how dainty and fragile they are," I said. "You build up muscles tossing calves into trucks."

"Tough girl," he said. "I'd better never offend you or you might flatten me with a right hook! What were you putting them on trucks for anyway?"

"Sending them off to be made into veal," I said matter-of-factly.

Ryan looked horrified. "What, those poor little babies?"

"That's what veal is," I said. "Calf meat. A rancher can't keep all the calves every year."

"Boy, I'd no idea I'd get myself mixed up with such a heartless person," Ryan said.

"You can't be sentimental about animals if you run a ranch," I said. "That's the first thing I learned. Believe me, I had quite a few bouts of tears and tantrums when I was little and fell in love with a special animal. My father never gave in to me, though. He said I had to learn that the world was a tough place."

Ryan nodded. "At least you had the right upbringing for dealing with me," he said.

"You'd better not try to get away from me," I said with a grin. "I used to be a whiz at calf roping when I was a kid!"

As we drove on, we left the neat fields and farms behind us. The road wound up a grassy slope. Snow-capped mountains were ahead of us, but down where we were everything was new and green and growing madly. Ryan stopped the car and we got out. The air smelled clean and fresh and full of the scent of spring flowers. Everywhere there were patches of bright color in the grass. Trees were bursting with bright new leaves and sprigs of blossom. All around us was the sound of running water as little streams made their way over waterfalls down to the creek in the valley bottom.

"It's amazing," I said to Ryan. "All this happened around me every year and I took it all for granted."

Ryan nodded. "It's amazing how much you take for granted when you have it."

He took my hand. We walked together up a winding path that followed one of the streams. The wind was in our faces. We could see it on the hill above, moving through the grass like a giant comb through hair. The ground under our feet was still moist and muddy and at each stop we left our footprints behind.

At the top of the hill we stood together, panting. Around us nothing was moving except the wind. We could hear it sighing. There was no other sound. I gazed at Ryan and raised my lips to be brushed with a gentle kiss. His eyes gazed down into mine, looking at me so intensely that it felt as if he were reaching into my soul.

Then he was kissing me, gently at first, then hungrily. Nothing mattered anymore. I was safe and secure in his arms and felt a great cloud of happiness envelop me. I wanted the moment to last forever, just like that, just me and Ryan, alone with the spring wind.

I don't know how long I stood there, wrapped in Ryan's arms, my head nestled into his shoulder, but suddenly I felt him stiffen.

"What's wrong?" I asked.

"Look!" he whispered. "Over there."

On the hill opposite was a group of wild horses, their manes and tails blowing majestically in the wind.

"Just think, King was one of those once," Ryan said. I don't know if they picked up the sound of his voice, but all at once they lifted their heads and galloped off across the hill, moving effortlessly with their tails streaming out behind them. We kept on watching long after the last one had disappeared over the crest.

"Do you think King still remembers what it was like to be free?" Ryan said as we walked back to the car. "Sometimes I wonder if we're doing the right thing in trying to tame him."

I turned and looked back at the empty hillside. Being free *was* wonderful, I thought. But wasn't there such a thing as too much freedom? It seemed almost the same as being alone—and I knew being alone was the emptiest feeling of all.

Chapter Eighteen

I didn't think about those wild horses again for a long time. Not until many things had happened to me I never imagined could happen. My thoughts right then were on getting King ready for his first horse show. It was in May and only three weeks away.

"What's the matter?" Ryan asked me one afternoon as we walked King slowly back to the stable.

"Nothing."

"Come on. Something's worrying you."

I shrugged my shoulders. "Oh, I'm just wondering if we're doing the right thing, entering King in a show this soon."

"But he's terrific, Eden," Ryan said, giving his golden flank a hearty slap. "Don't tell me

162

you've ever seen a horse who learned to jump this quickly. He's a natural."

"Yes, but he's not the most predictable horse, is he?" I asked. "You've never been to a horse show. I have. I've seen fat little ponies who suddenly go ga-ga when they see all those strange horses or tents flapping. I've watched horses who never do a thing wrong suddenly refuse to jump for no reason at all."

"I want to take the chance, Eden," Ryan said. "I know something could go wrong, but what's the worst thing that could happen?"

"King could bolt through the crowd, mow down a few kids, throw you off, and break your neck."

Ryan grinned. "Apart from that?" he asked. "I really feel I can handle him. He knows it, Eden. He knows I'm strong enough."

"But look at yesterday," I said. "He danced around for hours before he would go near a jump, then he ran past the wall twice."

"So he's not perfect yet."

"But what I'm saying is that there will be other horse shows. Are we rushing things a bit?"

"I'm racing against a clock, too," Ryan said. "Who knows how many more horse shows there might be? If my mother and my doctor find out about this one, I'm done for. Besides, we don't even know how long we have a horse."

He turned and saw my surprised face. "Well, we don't, do we?" he went on. "You said old

Bradley was going to sell King in the spring, and you've got to admit that King's completely broken now."

"Oh," I said. Like so many other unpleasant things, I had put that completely out of my mind. King was so much a part of our lives that I couldn't imagine what it would be like without him. Every afternoon when I arrived he would be peering out of his stall in the direction of the gate, waiting for me. As soon as he saw me he would toss his head up and down and nicker. If I dared to stop and greet another horse first he would neigh loudly, like a little kid yelling, "I'm here, I'm here." I realized now how much I had deluded myself into thinking he was my horse.

Mr. Bradley had never seen us work out with King, so he didn't know just how good King had become. We hadn't mentioned to him that we were entering King in a horse show, because Mr. Bradley would immediately decide that King would be worth a lot of money if we won. He must have realized that King no longer acted up when he was saddled and that he behaved like a civilized horse. But he never mentioned King's future, so I crossed my fingers and went on hoping that he would keep King around just because he was a beautiful animal who looked good at the head of a trail ride.

As the horse show approached I was so nervous and excited that I couldn't think about anything else. Trisha had said that she'd love to come and see me if I was ever in a horse-jumping competition. I felt really bad about not inviting her to this one. She had been so nice to me, and I didn't like keeping things from her. But I had promised Ryan that I wouldn't tell anyone at school about us. He was so paranoid about being tracked down again.

The last couple of days before the show, I tried to act normally at home, although my stomach was full of butterflies. I was more nervous than any time I had ridden Charlie. Even though I tried to be cool, I guess my parents noticed I was jittery.

"What's with you?" my father said.

"Nothing," I said. "Why?" I didn't want to tell Dad about the show. The arrival of spring had accomplished what I'd been trying to do for months. He had started to come out of his depression. He was beginning to spend time at the store; he needed to if he was ever to get it opened. I was afraid that if I got him interested in the show now he'd neglect the store.

"You're jumping all over the place like a newborn calf, that's why," he said. "You can't sit still for a minute."

"Oh," I said. "Exams at school coming up, I guess."

"In which case," my mother said, coming into the room, "I think you ought to spend a bit more time with your books and a bit less time at the stables."

"Oh, don't worry," I said. "I take my homework down there with me, and I do it when I'm not busy."

"Well, don't forget, your studies come first," she said. "I don't see how you can study if there's no proper table and chair to work at."

This conversation was obviously getting out of hand. To put a stop to it I said, "Hey, Dad, guess what? I saw some newborn calves a couple weeks ago."

"You did, where?"

"Oh, somewhere on the edge of town."

He nodded. "Late for calves," he said. "Still, they're higher up than we were. What breed were they?"

"Jerseys," I said. "They were really sweet."

"Jerseys," my father said and a faraway look came over his face. "Did I ever tell you about the time my dad kept Jerseys? That was back in the days when people didn't care about cholesterol and things and he wanted to improve the cream content in his milk. They were the nicest little animals. We had two calves who used to follow us about like dogs. Bonnie and Daisy. I can still remember them as if it were yesterday. I always thought that one day, when I retired . . ." His voice faded. Then he got up. "Won't do to sit around all day talking," he said. "I've got to get on that paint supplier." And he walked from the room.

The Friday before the show I went straight to the stables from school, so that I had extra

166

time to polish up the tack and braid King's mane and tail.

"What are you doing, playing hairdresser?" Ryan asked, peering in at me over the top of the stall.

"I'm making him look nice," I said. "It's hard work. He has so much mane."

"I thought he looked nice enough before," Ryan said.

"You don't know a thing about horse shows," I said.

"So you keep reminding me," he said teasingly. "What am I supposed to do now, sit and admire him?"

"Give that saddle another rub over," I said. "And polish your boots while you're at it."

"Yes, ma'am!" Ryan said, saluting.

"I'm sorry," I said, looking up and grinning. "I guess I'm nervous today."

"That's OK," he said. "I am, too. But don't worry. King and I won't let you down. You've got yourself a classy team here, you know!"

"I know," I said. I leaned out of the horse box and took Ryan's face in my hands.

I was about to kiss him when King's powerful head thrust between us.

"The other man in your life is madly jealous," Ryan said, laughing.

"All right, I get the message," I said, rubbing King's face. "I'll finish your hair first. Honestly, you men are more vain than any woman!"

Chapter Nineteen

I met Ryan outside the stables very early that Saturday morning, long before Mr. Bradley was due there. We had told him we were going to take King for a good long exercise, because he was getting skittish again. I don't know what he would have done if he'd found out the exercise was twenty miles away at a horse show. We had rented a horse trailer, which Ryan had conveniently left a couple of blocks away so that nobody saw us go.

"Made it safely." Ryan sighed as we reached the trailer. "I felt like a thief, didn't you?"

We ran into a slight problem when we tried to put King into the trailer. Obviously he had bad memories of the last time he had ridden in one and flatly refused to get in. In the end, I had to walk him in, talking to him every step of the way. It was only then that I realized how much he trusted me, because as I spoke he stopped trembling and rested his elegant head against my shoulder. But he started to throw a fit every time I tried to get out, so I wound up riding in the trailer all the way to the show with King leaning on me.

Finally we arrived at the field, which was all decked out with green and white flags. Ryan drove over the grass to park at the end of a long row of trailers.

"I'm exhausted," I complained as Ryan opened the trailer to get us out. "And carsick. These things sway around a lot."

"I thought I drove very carefully," Ryan said.

"For you, you did," I agreed. "But there were a lot of fumes back here, and it didn't help having King squashing me all the time."

"Poor old fellow, you didn't like it, did you," Ryan said soothingly, leading King down the ramp.

"I like that," I growled. "You don't say 'poor old fellow' to me. I guess I don't matter around here."

Ryan looked back and grinned. "You don't look like a poor old fellow," he said. "In fact you look pretty good—for a horse trainer!"

"I'll deal with you later," I threatened.

He raised an eyebrow. "I can't wait," he said.

We joked and kidded around as we gave King a final brush down and brought out his saddle and bridle. Neither of us wanted to admit how tense we were feeling, and our silly insults helped break the tension.

It was a chilly morning and mist hung like wisps of cotton across the low-lying field. The sun had not yet risen above the mist so the world around us was gray. Triangular flags fluttered around the edge of the main ring. To its side were two big, bright green-and-white tents, one for officials and another for refreshments. Music was already blaring from a loudspeaker. Little kids dressed in brand-new black velvet riding helmets and clean black jackets strode earnestly past us, swishing at the grass with new leather crops, or leading willing ponies behind them. In the practice ring a woman was working a large bay on dressage, reining in to walk backward, then moving into an extended trot in circles. The horse moved with beautiful, fluid grace, and I wondered if I could ever bring King to that degree of training and perfection.

The bay finished warming up, and a pretty little Arab mare with a serious young boy on her back trotted up and down in the ring a few times. He was joined by a woman—his mother, probably—in a pale mink coat, giving him some last minute pointers on how to ride.

"Are you going to stand there all day doing nothing?" Ryan demanded. "Shouldn't we saddle him up? Come on, you know all about these things."

"Sorry," I said, snapping to attention. "No,

don't put his saddle on yet. It might not be our turn for hours. I was just enjoying being around so many horses again. Doesn't it smell good?"

"It smells horsey," Ryan said, wrinkling his nose. "I don't know about good!"

"Oh, but it does smell good," I said. "It reminds me of when Charlie and I used to . . ." I broke off. "I'd better not stand around talking," I said. "We have to check in and get a program."

As we stood there with King between us, it suddenly hit me that this was the big test. If King did well that day, maybe all sorts of good things would follow. Maybe I could persuade Mr. Bradley to let me train him for one of the big shows, like the one at the State Fair this summer.

I guess Ryan was thinking of other things. That day was a time for him to prove that he hadn't let himself be beaten.

King stood between us like a statue, sniffing uneasily at the scents of strange horses. Every now and then he nuzzled at my sleeve, as if to say, "This is going to be OK, isn't it?" He seemed relieved when, at nine o'clock, we were allowed to walk him around the course. King behaved beautifully, nodding with interest as we showed him each jump.

"These first two brushwoods are really easy," I told Ryan. "But don't let him relax, because you've got those yellow poles with the geraniums on either side of them right after, and you'll need to be going pretty hard for that.'"

"What about the water jump?" Ryan asked. "I've never tried one of those before."

"It'll be a piece of cake for King," I said. "Just let him loose."

"Let's just hope I can collect him again before the triple," Ryan said, grinning nervously. "Otherwise we'll be in Boulder before we know where we are."

"That triple's going to be really tough for him," I pointed out to Ryan. "He'll want to jump those first two together if you're not careful. See, there's only room for one small stride between them."

"And those uneven bars," Ryan said, pointing. "He doesn't like those much because he can't judge his height too well."

"You're right," I said. "Especially since you have to swing him around hard after the wall to make an approach."

Just then a girl in a very expensive-looking riding habit strolled over to us, leading a beautiful bay horse behind her.

"Hello," she said, eyeing us both. "I don't think I've seen you around here before."

"You haven't," I said. "This is our first show here."

An amused glance flickered across her face. "Oh, this is all new to you then. How exciting!" she said with exaggerated enthusiasm. "Well, don't hope for too much on your first time out. There's some high-class competition today. I can name at least three people who have a chance of taking that blue ribbon away from me." When we smiled politely and didn't answer she lost interest in us. "Well, good luck then," she said, casting a sidelong glance at King. "Pretty palomino. Bit big for a jumper, though, isn't he?" She drifted away again.

"I'd have liked to push her down in that mud over there," Ryan said. "Spoiled little—"

"Forget it," I said. "She wasn't worth it."

"But why didn't you tell her about all your trophies up in Wyoming? You let her think we were complete beginners."

"Right," I said. "That way we'll surprise everyone if we win. You meet a lot of people like her at horse shows. They specialize in being catty."

Our event—the senior English jumping competition—wasn't due to start until later in the morning. While we waited we made sure King stayed warm with his blanket on, watching impatiently while some little kids put ponies through their paces and bigger kids did some western barrel races. All the time the crowd was getting bigger. The smell of hot dogs cooking competed with the warm smell of the horses. Neither of us had eaten that day but neither of us was hungry.

Finally the riders for our event were called to the officials' tent. We drew an early number because we were unknown, so Ryan got up on King and warmed him up gently. Again

King behaved perfectly, and I heard lots of comments about the "pretty new palomino."

Suddenly the bell rang and the first horse entered the ring. Both horse and rider were nervous and they ended up with hundreds of faults. The next rider was the same. Then it was King's turn. He looked wonderful as he came into the ring at a controlled trot. His powerful muscles shimmered as if he couldn't wait to get to work. He took each jump as if it were merely a twig lying in his path.

I stood there gripping the fence and not even daring to breathe. I was lifting King mentally over every fence. But after he swung around to take those uneven bars with a foot to spare, I began to relax. I even looked around to see if I could catch a glimpse of the snobby girl's face, but she was out behind, warming up.

Everything went perfectly until the triple jump. I could tell King was headed for disaster by the way he lengthened his stride. Ryan was relaxing, too, and obviously didn't realize that King was going too fast. They came up to the triple, and King made a mighty bound, trying to clear the first two parts in one jump. I heard the spectators give a horrified gasp, then a second of admiration as he came down, almost clear of the second bars, just clipping the top rail with his hind feet. The rail bounced and fell. Four faults. He landed all wrong for the third part and leaped almost vertically to clear it by a fraction of an inch.

Then miraculously, Ryan fought to collect him before the last two hurdles, a big wall and brushwood fence. They made it home to a big round of applause from the crowd.

"You were terrific," I said, taking King's reins as Ryan slid from his back.

"King was terrific," Ryan said. "I blew it. I should have realized we were coming at the triple too fast." He shook his head. "Crazy horse—did you ever see one who thought he could jump two fences at once?" He turned to slip King some carrot sticks.

"But only one fence down is very good," I said. "You should be pleased with yourself."

"But I've already knocked us out of the jump-off," he said. "I really wanted to go home with a ribbon."

"So did I," I said. "But at least we've proved to ourselves that King is trained enough for a horse show. There will be plenty more, if I can just talk Mr. Bradley into letting us enter."

As we were putting King's blanket on, the girl came up to us again. "Nice try," she said. "You almost made it. But perhaps you didn't realize that that was a triple jump. You're not supposed to take the first two fences at once." She laughed a high, silly laugh.

"Thank you, I'll remember next time," Ryan said with forced politeness.

"It comes from being new at this," the girl said sweetly, flirting with Ryan. "What you need is a good trainer. Do you live around here?"

"I already have my trainer, thank you," Ryan explained.

"But you need someone with a little class," she said, "who can share her experience with you."

"Oh, believe me, my trainer is great at sharing experience," Ryan said. I turned around to rub down King so that she wouldn't see me giggling.

"Well, I'm glad of that," she said. "I'd make sure your stable girl rubs him down properly. Looks like she's only doing a halfhearted job to me."

"I'll get out my whip," Ryan said. "Nice talking to you—"

"Melanie," she said sweetly. "I've got to go. I'm on soon. See you later, maybe?"

As soon as she had gone we both collapsed in helpless giggles.

"I needed that," Ryan said. "It made me realize that winning isn't everything. It's much more fun to be us and have a good time!"

"Maybe you'd have a better time with Melanie, later?" I asked teasingly.

"Nah," he said, shaking his head. "I can't trust my stable girl to do a good job on my horse unless I keep an eye on her every minute."

As I was undoing the girth straps a large man with an official's badge on his riding jacket walked over to us. "I don't think you've got time to fool around with girths now," he said. "You should be over there."

"Over where?"

"In the ring, of course," he said as if we were idiots.

"You must have us mixed up with someone else," Ryan said.

The man frowned. "You're number three, aren't you? You're in the jump-off."

"But I didn't get a clear round," Ryan said.

"Neither did anyone else," the man answered. "Good luck. Nice-looking horse you've got there. He's not for sale, by any chance, is he?"

"No," I said firmly. "He's not for sale." Hastily I tightened the girth straps again, and Ryan swung himself into the saddle.

Two horses jumped before us, including Melanie's. She was doing wonderfully until her horse stopped dead at the wall and she went sailing over it. For some reason I found that very satisfying! Strangely enough she didn't come over and talk to us as she rode, red faced, out of the ring.

Then it was Ryan's turn. He and King moved around the ring perfectly, in total harmony, as they sailed effortlessly over the jumps. This time when they came up to the triple they took the small stride between the first two parts. *They're going to do it,* I thought excitedly. *They're going to win!* I closed my eyes and imagined boarding a plane with Ryan and King as we flew first to New York and San Francisco to compete, then to the Olympic trials.

I opened them again as King came to the last three fences. Ryan bent low over King's mane, which I hadn't seen him do before, but King didn't seem to notice. He cleared them all easily.

I rushed over and threw my arms around King's neck. "You were wonderful, both of you. My clever precious thing. I knew you could do it!"

I looked up to Ryan. "Don't sit up there letting everyone admire you. You can get down now. You've won!" I called.

"Eden," Ryan rasped in a funny voice. "Help me." Before I could do anything he slithered off King and fell in a heap to the ground.

"Ryan!" I screamed. "What's the matter?"

"I can't move," Ryan whispered in a strange, slurred voice. "After the triple I couldn't use my hands—I couldn't hold the reins. King jumped everything by himself." He closed his eyes. "Good old King," he murmured.

Suddenly people were crowding around us. A couple of paramedics pushed me out of the way, an ambulance appeared, and they started to load him onto a stretcher. Ryan was still half-conscious, obviously dazed from the fall. "Don't leave me, Eden," he said.

"Where are your folks, son?" the paramedics asked kindly.

They fished his I.D. out of a pocket and someone rushed to the phone.

"Can I come with him?" I asked.

"Are you a relative?" they asked me. When I

shook my head, one of the paramedics said, "Sorry, miss. We're taking him to Mercy Hospital. You can follow in your car."

"But he wants me with him!" I pleaded.

"Sorry, miss. Now, out of the way, everybody. Lift him gently."

I watched helplessly as Ryan was carried through the crowd. I thought I heard him call my name. Everyone melted away and I was left alone with King.

"What are we going to do now?" I asked him, rubbing my face against his soft neck. "How am I going to get you home?" I thought of driving Ryan's car with the stick shift, pulling a trailer full of horse behind me, and I knew there was no way I could do it. Besides having been too busy at the stables to get my license, I was too nervous to drive. My hands were shaking, and I could even feel my knees trembling.

King stayed close to me as if he understood. We stood there in a dream as someone brought over a blue ribbon and pinned it on King's bridle. People came up to ask questions and congratulate us, then they walked off again.

What am I going to do? I wailed to myself. Then I remembered a day when I was about ten years old. I had fallen off Charlie, and he had run home without me. I had started walking but my ankle hurt me. I remembered feeling alone and scared, miles from my home. I didn't want to call home because that would be admitting defeat. But finally I couldn't walk another step. I hobbled into the little grocery store and called my dad. "Come and get me," I had sobbed. "I need you right now."

I hadn't asked my dad to do anything for me since his attack, but now I had no choice. I put some coins into the pay phone outside the ring. "Daddy, can you come and get me?" I asked. "I need you right now."

Chapter Twenty

The following afternoon Ryan lay in a narrow white hospital bed with the sheets tucked in crisply around him. His eyes were closed, and his face was almost as pale as the white sheets themselves.

I stood in the doorway, fighting back my tears. *How could I have been so dumb?* I thought. *I knew he was very sick but I pretended to myself that he wasn't. But he never forgot it.*

I remembered now how he had told me he was racing against a clock and how there might not be any more carnivals. Each time I had laughed off his fears. I realized now how selfish that had been. Maybe he wanted to talk about those fears, but I'd shut him up by telling him I didn't want to hear any more gloomy thoughts. *I guess I really only thought about me,* I thought unhappily. *Just because so many bad things had happened to me, I didn't want any more bad things to think about.*

I tiptoed over to him and touched his right hand. "Ryan," I whispered, "please get well again, and I'll make it up to you. I told you I loved you, but I don't think I loved you enough. Now I know that I do."

Ryan's face didn't change a bit. His hand was cold.

"People do not die from multiple sclerosis. It is not a life-threatening disease," I kept chanting to myself over and over. That was what the medical dictionary had said. I hadn't bothered to look it up until I got home from the horse show. I hadn't wanted to know the horrible details before. Now I knew that it could flare up at any time and affect almost any part of the body, including the eyes and the speech mechanisms. It could paralyze muscles, make hands shake violently, but people did recover from the acute stages, although their condition generally got worse and worse. I also learned that people suffering from MS should not do too much and should stay away from stress. Maybe I was the one who helped cause this attack. After all, there couldn't be much more emotional and physical stress than a big horse competition.

But would I have talked Ryan out of entering it? After debating it in my mind, I realized there was nothing I could have done to stop him. It had given him something to be excited about. Now at least he knew he had been a riding champion once. That would make him feel good for the rest of his life.

A nurse came in silently. "You might want to come back later," she said gently. "He had a pretty bad fall. He's been sedated, and he won't wake up for a while."

"I'll stay," I said. "I know he'll want to see me when he wakes up."

"Are you his girlfriend?" she asked with a friendly smile. When I nodded she shook her head. "Well, you should have stopped him from being so foolish. Imagine going horseback riding in his condition!"

"He won the blue ribbon," I said. "That was important to him."

She sighed and shook her head again. "You young people," she muttered as she walked out.

Again I was left alone in the white room. There was no color anywhere, and if I hadn't been wearing a red sweater, I'd have wondered if I'd strayed into a nightmare world where everything was white. The world was unreal enough as it was. Strange messages echoed down the halls outside. Sometimes feet ran past. The hospital smells of disinfectant, polish, ether, and sickness totally engulfed me. They stuck in my nose and throat, making my head swirl and adding to the unreality.

Nothing had made any sense since the day before. My father had been wonderful, though. He had come straight over, taking charge as soon as he appeared.

"What happened to Ryan? Did he take a bad fall?" my father asked. He put an arm around me to stop my nervous shivering.

"Yes, but he finished the round first," I said, not wanting my father to think that Ryan was a bad rider. "He won. Look, here's the blue ribbon. It was King's first show, and they won. Wasn't that terrific?" I could hear myself babbling on as if I were afraid of one moment of silence.

"Eden," my father said firmly, "don't worry too much. He looks like a tough kid to me. Kids your age recover so easily from broken bones. We'll take the horse back where it belongs, and then we'll call the hospital."

"Thanks, Dad," I muttered, wishing with all my heart that it was just broken bones we were dealing with.

Dad was terrific. He helped me get a tired, bad-tempered King into the trailer.

"Phew," he said, when we had finally put the pin into place. "Don't tell me this is one of the riding school horses! He'd make mincemeat of any novice rider."

"He's not a regular school horse," I said. "He was only half-broken when we got him,

184

but he's much better now. He just senses all the tension."

"Beautiful horse," my father said. "Why didn't you tell us about this show? I'd have loved to come and watch."

"You were so busy with the store," I explained. "I didn't want to do anything to interfere. Besides, it was their first show, both Ryan and King. I wasn't sure how things would go, so I didn't want anyone watching."

My father gave me a hug, then helped me into the car. "Your interfering helped get me back on my feet," he said.

I was surprised and thrilled. So all my nagging, my worrying, hadn't been entirely useless! I'd thought it was just the warm weather that had gotten him out of the house. But he'd been listening to me all that time. Managing a smile, I reached across and touched his hand. "I'm so glad you're here, Daddy," I said. "Let's go home."

As soon as I walked in the door I called the hospital. They told me that nobody could see Ryan till morning. All I could get out of them was that he was resting comfortably and that his doctor would see him the next day.

For the longest time I paced around the apartment like a caged animal, then I decided to go down to the library and read everything I could about MS. I had to know whether Ryan was going to get better again.

Inside the library I bumped into Trisha, who was surrounded by mounds of books.

"Hi, Eden," she called, waving to me. "Do you believe this English assignment? Twentieth-century American poets. Yuck." She patted the chair next to hers. "Here, have a seat."

"Er, not now, Trisha," I said. "I'm in a hurry."

She looked at my face, then asked, "Eden, is something wrong?"

"N-no. Everything's fine," I mumbled.

She shook her head. "Something is wrong," she said gently. "Sometimes it helps to talk about things."

"But I promised I wouldn't," I said hopelessly.

"Are you in some kind of trouble?" she whispered. "I'd really like to help. And I promise I won't tell another soul, if that's what you're worrying about."

I sank down onto the hard library chair beside her. "It's not me," I said. "It's Ryan."

"Ryan?" she asked, surprised. "You mean Ryan Benson? Has he been annoying you or something?"

"Nothing like that," I said. "We've been going together for a while now." I caught my breath. "He's very sick, Trisha," I whispered. "I didn't realize how sick until today. He has multiple sclerosis, but he seemed so well until today. He fell off a horse and he's sort of paralyzed and I don't even know if he's going to be OK. Trisha, what am I going to do?"

She was looking at me hard, as if she was trying to take all this in. "So Ryan left school because he was sick," she said, shaking her head as if she couldn't believe it. "Typical Ryan, of course. I can imagine him doing that. But how dumb—everyone liked him in school. Everyone would have wanted to help him."

"He was afraid of everyone's pity," I said. "That's why he wouldn't even let me tell my parents about it."

"I'm not talking about pity," Trisha said sharply. "I'm talking about friendship. When things are bad you need friends to help you get through."

"You're right," I said. "I realize that now, but Ryan was so afraid. He didn't like people to know how afraid he was, so he shut himself away. Maybe now we can help him see how wrong he was!"

"Have you been to see him yet?" Trisha asked.

"They won't let me in now," I said. "But I'm going first thing in the morning, whether they let me or not."

"You want me to walk home with you now?" Trisha asked, piling her books together. "My folks are out. We could sit and talk if you'd like."

"Yes," I said. "I'd like that. But first I've got to find out everything I can about MS. I have to know what to expect."

So for the next half hour I browsed through medical encyclopedias, reading everything I could find. I kept taking out one after the other, just in case one mentioned that people

187

sometimes died, in spite of what the others said.

After that Trisha and I walked home together and we sat talking until pretty late. I felt as if a great load had been taken off my shoulders. When Ryan was well again, I'd make him understand how much easier it was when you had friends.

I called the hospital first thing in the morning and was told that Ryan spent a comfortable night and was resting.

"What's the news on Ryan?" my father asked as soon as I hung up the phone. "Did he break anything?"

"They didn't say so," I said.

"So I expect they'll let him out today," my father said encouragingly.

"All the same," I said, staring past him and out of the window, "I think I'll go down to the hospital. Just in case they don't let him out."

"Do you want a ride?" my father asked.

"It's OK. I can take the bus," I said.

"So you don't want me to drive you anymore," he said, looking hurt.

"I don't want to impose," I said.

"What do you mean?" he muttered. "I'm still your father."

"OK, then, I'd love a ride," I said. "I'll get my coat."

The hospital had looked so big and new and unfriendly that I had almost taken my father up on his offer to come in with me. But I had a feeling he'd start asking Ryan all the details of his accident, and I didn't want Ryan to be mad at me. So I told him I'd be just fine by myself, and he left.

I really wished he was there with me, though. Every minute seemed so long. There was a clock on the wall that gave a loud tick every thirty seconds as the hand jumped forward. I sat there, holding my breath and waiting for the next tick. I jumped each time, even though I was expecting it. How long could I sit there by Ryan's side? What if Ryan didn't wake up for hours and hours?

My vigil was soon interrupted when I heard the *tap-tap-tap* of high-heeled shoes coming down the hall. The door was thrust open, and a strange woman stood there.

"Oh, I'm sorry. I must have the wrong room," she said, seeing me sitting by the bed. Then she focused on the sleeping patient. "No, I don't," she said and looked at me again. "Who are you?" she demanded.

She was tall and blond, enough like Ryan to make me realize right away that she was his mother. But whereas his blond hair flopped into his eyes and was the color of light corn, hers was set into stiff curls and looked straight out of a box of Lady Clairol. Her eyes were the same blue as his, but had none of the sparkle.

I got up feeling guilty, like someone who'd sneaked into a movie through a side entrance.

"You must be Ryan's mother," I said, managing my best smile. "I'm Eden Harrison, Ryan's friend from the riding stable."

The severe look didn't melt one bit. "He never mentioned a special friend," she said suspiciously. Then an incredulous look crossed her face. "Don't tell me you're the horse trainer?"

"That's me."

"But I had no idea," she said. "I always assumed you were a much older person. Ryan never described you at all. In fact, he was very reluctant to talk about you, so I gathered you didn't get along together." She walked over to her son, stood looking down at him, then bent to brush back the lock of hair that had fallen across his forehead. "What an idiotic thing to do," she went on, looking up at me. "Still, I suppose you had no idea he was so sick. He won't tell anyone. If only I'd known, but then I thought he was just walking horses on trail rides. But it turns out the idiot boy was trying to make one jump when he fell off."

I felt anger boiling up inside me. "Your son is a fantastic rider," I said. "He jumped a clear round in his first show. He's very gifted."

"He's also, unfortunately, very sick," she said. "And the sooner he accepts that and starts living the right sort of life, the better. I've been going out of my mind with worry ever since the disease was diagnosed, trying to keep him at home and safe. But he won't stay put—just like his father, always rushing off to do something dangerous. In a way this fall is very lucky. It'll let him see how foolish he's been to attempt this sort of nonsense. There will be no more horse jumping from now on."

My face must have reflected my anger at her one-sided thinking. Didn't she realize her overprotectiveness could be just as dangerous to him?

She frowned at me. "I don't suppose you knew he has multiple sclerosis," she said. "His doctors have told him a hundred times that he mustn't do anything strenuous or he'll bring on an acute attack. We made him stop skiing last year and now he does this. I'll end up an invalid myself with the worry." She glanced down at Ryan. "Has he slept all morning?" she asked.

"Since I've been here," I said.

"In that case I think I'll pop along to the cafeteria and get some coffee," she said. "I don't think you need to wait around any longer, miss. The doctors told me they wanted him to rest today." She looked as if she might have me thrown out by force.

"I'll just stay a few minutes more," I said, fighting back a desire to be rude to her.

She sighed, turned her back on me, and walked out of the room.

As soon as she was gone I leaned over and flicked the lock of hair back across Ryan's forehead. As I did so he opened his eyes.

They focused on me, looking brighter than ever against the paleness of his surroundings. His face creased into a smile. "Eden?" he asked.

"Right here."

"Oh, I thought I heard my mother's voice, but it turned out to be you," he said, stumbling over the words. "I can't make my mouth obey me."

"It's OK. I can understand," I said. "How are you feeling?"

"Apart from feeling like I've been kicked in the back of the neck, I'm fine," he mumbled. "And yesterday I couldn't move my right hand. Wait a minute." He looked down, concentrating on his fingers. His face turned pink. Then he fell back on the pillow. "Rats," he said. "I still can't move it. They keep telling me that any paralysis will go away. They'd better be right because I need that right hand."

"I'll make it better with a kiss," I said, bending down and kissing it.

"Hey, that was great, I think I felt it," he said. "You could try kissing more of me and see if I feel that."

"I've been warned very strongly that you are not to be excited," I said firmly.

"I know," he said, staring up at the ceiling and giving a big sigh. "They lectured me last night. Both my mother and the doctor. Not to do anything strenuous again. Not to get myself upset. Take things easy. Take up chess." There was a pause. Then he said,

"You know, Eden, they won't let me ride a horse again."

"Your mother told me."

"'You met my mother?" he asked, wrinkling his forehead. "How did it go?"

"She told me I didn't look like a horse trainer and that it was my fault her son was sick," I said. "Otherwise we got along fine."

Ryan grinned. "She'd like to lock me away in a cardboard box," he said. "She thinks I'm doing it to spite her—like my father leaving her. But she's not a bad old thing!"

I grinned. "I get the impression she wouldn't like to be called an old thing!"

"She takes good care of herself, I admit," he said. "But when you come from a good-looking family like me, you have to make the most of what nature has given you—just so that all the regular, ugly human beings can get joy from gazing at us."

"Today would be a good day to tickle you," I said, glaring down at him, "because you couldn't stop me. But I'm not that mean and I don't want to excite you. All I can say is you wait till you're well again, and I'll teach you a lesson."

"I can't wait," he said. "I'm bored with lying in bed. When do you think they'll let me go home?"

"I've no idea," I said. "But I think you could recover just as well at home."

I left when his mother came back. I decided that the two of us fighting for his attention

193

wouldn't be a good thing for someone who shouldn't be under stress. So I slipped out, but I felt in a good mood all the way home. Ryan wasn't going to die. He could still laugh and joke and was itching to get back home. Everything was going to be fine.

Chapter Twenty-one

I sensed something was wrong as soon as I phoned the hospital the next morning. The nurse on duty told me Ryan had been transferred. "Ready to leave?" I asked brightly.

"Oh, no, dear," she said. "Didn't they tell you what happened last night?"

"No," I said, cold fear creeping up my spine.

"He has pneumonia," she said calmly as if she was telling me about the weather, "and a collapsed lung. He's in the intensive care unit now."

"Can you transfer me there?" I asked, hearing my voice quiver.

"You won't be able to talk to him today," she said. "He's a very sick young man. Why don't you call again this evening?"

There was a click as the line went dead. I hung up the phone slowly.

"So how's he doing?" my father asked, coming into the room with the newspaper under his arm. "Going home today?"

"No, he's not," I whispered. "He's really sick. He's got pneumonia now and his lung collapsed and they won't let me talk to him."

"That's a strange turn of events," my father said. "You don't usually hear of young healthy people getting pneumonia after a fall. Still, I expect he'll shake it off quickly."

"Yes," I said, looking down at my hands. "I'm sure he'll be just fine."

My father put down the paper firmly and walked over to me. "Eden," he said, laying his hands on both my shoulders. "Don't shut us out all the time. I haven't seen you looking like this since Grandma Harrison died. You can talk to your old father, you know. I have all the time in the world to listen, and it's a lot better to share."

"But I promised him I wouldn't," I pleaded.

"Wouldn't what, punkin?" he asked, calling me by the pet name he hadn't used in years.

"Wouldn't tell you about him."

"Tell us what?"

"That he's very sick, Dad."

"But they can cure pneumonia easily these days."

I shook my head. "No, you don't understand. He was sick before. He has an incurable disease—multiple sclerosis. It's just going to get worse and worse. And the terrible thing is that he shouldn't have done anything strenuous." I looked up into my father's tired, kind eyes. "I helped him train a horse to jump, Dad. I feel so terrible."

"Hey, punkin," Dad said. "Don't cry." His arms came around me in a surprisingly strong bear hug. I stood there for a long while, my head resting against his shoulder, feeling safe and secure. This was my dad again, the one who used to pick me up when I fell down.

"Daddy," I whispered, "I'm glad you're here."

"I've always been here, Eden," he said. "Your mom and I have been worried about you these past few months. Sometimes it seemed that you were trying to shut us out of your life—as if you'd never forgive us for taking you away from Wyoming."

"I didn't dare show you how unhappy I was feeling," I said. "Or how scared I was that you might die, Daddy."

"There were times when I thought that might be the best thing for all of us," he said slowly.

"How can you say such a thing?" I blurted out. "What would Mom and I do without you?"

Dad looked past me, out the window. "When they told me my heart was damaged and that I'd have to sell the ranch, I lay there and asked myself, 'Why bother?' That ranch was everything to me. It was a bad piece of land nobody wanted, but I worked at it and it ended up being a pretty fair little spread. And my cattle were fine, healthy animals, weren't they? I was proud of my cattle."

Suddenly it was as if I were seeing through his eyes for the first time. Here he'd been shut up in a little apartment, only allowed to watch TV, popping pills every few hours that made him dopey. I slipped my arm through his. "These last months must have been pretty bad for you, Dad," I said.

He smiled. "I thought I'd go crazy, Eden," he said. "I'd watch your mother rushing out to her job and you to your riding, and I'd say to myself, 'Well, you useless old fool, why don't you just stop breathing right now. They don't need you anymore.' But then I realized that maybe a hardware store was just a beginning and maybe there were still a lot of sweet things in life to look forward to—like your graduation, seeing you through college. We're going to make it, Eden, you and I."

"You bet, Dad," I said, wiping away a tear with the back of my hand.

"Once we get that store going, Eden, once we get an income again, and if I'm feeling fit, we can put a manager in the store and buy a bit of property on the outskirts of town. Enough room for a horse and a few chickens and some vegetables. I'd like that, wouldn't you?"

"Yes, Dad," I said. "I'd like that a lot."

"So give your old father a smile, Eden," he said, taking my face in his hands. "And don't worry too much. I bet Ryan's a lot tougher than those hospital people think. If he can learn to jump horses in spite of a terrible disease, he must have a lot of fight in him."

I nodded and wiped the tears from my cheek.

"Why don't I run you down to that hospital this evening?" he went on. "Seeing you might be good for the boy."

"I'd like to go, even if they won't let me see him."

"And why don't you take the day off from school—you won't concentrate, anyway. Go on down to the stables. Remember how riding Charlie always used to make you feel better?"

"You're right," I said, jumping up suddenly. "Will you call in for me? I've just remembered that I didn't exercise King yesterday. He's so skittish if he doesn't get a good gallop. I'd better go before he kicks his stall down."

"You do that," my father said. "That'll take your mind off worrying. Me, I've got to get those shelves fitted. They start deliveries of supplies next week, and I need someone to paint a sign for us. No peace for the wicked, eh?"

As he walked out of the room I noticed that he no longer shuffled his feet.

King gave me a very haughty stare as I came across the yard as if to say, "Where were you yesterday?"

"It's just you and me today, old buddy," I said as I saddled him. He definitely sensed that Ryan wasn't around, because he kept looking at the gate. He was uneasy, too, shifting nervously from foot to foot the way he hadn't done in weeks.

I was just ready to mount him when Mr. Bradley showed up. "No school today?" he asked.

"Not for me," I said.

"So where's young Ryan?" he asked. "Haven't seen him around for a couple of days."

"He's in the hospital, Mr. Bradley," I said. "He's very sick with a collapsed lung. He won't be riding again."

"Oh, that's too bad," he said, almost looking upset. "I hope you don't decide to quit on me because he's not here. I quite enjoy our fights."

I swung myself up onto King's back. "Me, too," I replied.

"So he won't be here to ride the stallion anymore," Mr. Bradley remarked, nodding to himself. "Still, he did a good job. You both did a good job. You reckon he's ready to sell now?"

"I guess so," I said miserably.

"I'll find out when the next sale's coming up," he said, shuffling off as if I didn't exist any longer.

I rode King slowly down the grassy path. "You knew this was going to happen," I said to myself. "You knew that he was going to

200

sell King someday. At least he's a finely trained horse now. He can go to somebody like the people at that show. That man wanted to buy him—he'd treat him well."

I looked down at King's cascading mane, his delicate ears, and the wonderful arch of his neck. It seemed impossible to imagine my days without him. Maybe I could take him on the rest of the show circuit myself, maybe I could persuade Mr. Bradley to keep him and sponsor me. I even went through crazy schemes to earn enough money to buy him and board him in Bradley's field, but I couldn't come up with a crazy enough plan to make that kind of money.

We reached the beginning of the woodland trail. King kept looking back, surprised that we weren't heading toward the practice ring. I urged him on. He hesitated and I sensed he was waiting for Ryan. However much I loved him, he knew Ryan was boss. He had become Ryan's horse. Would he ever take directions from me the way he had obeyed Ryan? I gave him a firm kick. He looked at me, surprised, then broke into a graceful trot. I increased the pace. We started moving faster and faster. The trees all around us were bursting with new leaves, so that we couldn't see what was around the next bend. But I didn't care. I needed to go fast, just like Ryan and his sports car, as if going fast enough would blot out all the pain and worry.

A couple of miles along the trail we swung

around a sharp curve and there was the big gate, locked as it had been once before. Part of me was tempted to jump it. I heard a little voice whispering, "Go on, try it. See if you can do what Ryan did." Then the sensible part of me fought with the little voice. "Don't be dumb. If the horse jumps it badly he'll break a leg."

I applied pressure on the reins at the last minute. King came to a stop right before the gate. It was the ultimate test of his obedience and proved to me beyond a doubt that he was a perfectly trained horse, ready to sell.

"Come on, King, let's go home," I said. "I've had enough for today."

We were both content to walk slowly back along the trail.

Chapter Twenty-two

Dad drove me to the hospital that night but, as predicted, they wouldn't let me near Ryan. I did see his mother, though, and asked her to call me if she got any news about him.

"I'll certainly be happy to give you news," she said, looking at me coldly. "But I think it'd be wrong to introduce outsiders into his room before he's completely well again." I think she thought I was responsible for smuggling the pneumonia germ into his room.

So I had to go home again and spend a night that seemed to last a hundred hours. In the morning I had to go to school, but I stumbled around like a zombie, not noticing a thing that was going on around me.

"What's with you today?" Renee asked, grabbing my arm as we came out of English. "Mr.

Hollis had to tell you to pay attention twice. It looked like you were a million miles away."

"Just got some things on my mind," I said.

"Problems at home or boyfriend trouble?" she asked.

"Neither really," I began, turning away from her so she couldn't see my face.

"Eden, forget it," she interrupted. "It's really none of my business. My friends all tell me I have a big mouth. But I hate to see anyone unhappy, and I can tell you're really down."

"I have a friend who's pretty sick," I said. "I'm worried about him."

"That's too bad," Renee said kindly. "Is there anything I can do?"

I managed a smile. "'There's nothing anyone can do, except wait. That's the bad part."

"'Well, I'm here if you need me," she said. "After all, that's what friends are for, isn't it?"

"Thanks," I said. I longed to tell her at that moment, but I couldn't. After all, I had promised Ryan and I couldn't betray his trust right now.

I managed to get through the rest of the day. Right after school I called the hospital. Ryan was making slight progress but he still couldn't have any visitors. Dad persuaded me to come down to the store with him while he took a few measurements.

It was the first time I had been down at the store in a couple of weeks and I was amazed at the change. The shelves were in, the walls were brightly painted, and some of the hardware stock was already on display.

While I was still exclaiming, he led me upstairs. "There's a surprise for you," he said. He took me to a room in the apartment upstairs with pretty flowery wallpaper and two closets with a built-in vanity between them.

"We decided to rent this apartment as soon as it came vacant as a surprise for you. We can move in soon," my dad said behind me. "Your mother has a white fluffy rug and custom drapes to match the wallpaper on order. This will be your room."

"But, Dad, it must have cost a fortune," I said, feeling guilty about the way I had complained and criticized.

He smiled. "Lucky your ma gets a discount at that fancy store of hers—and she gets first pick of the seconds. She wanted you to have a nice room of your own. She always dreamed of having one when she was a girl, but then she always had to share with three sisters. We could never afford a pretty room for you out at the ranch, so she's really tried hard to make this one perfect."

I felt a lump come into the back of my throat. My mother, who hardly ever showed any emotion, who was quietly efficient, had dreams of her own that never came true. She needed my love as much as my father did.

That evening Ryan's mother phoned. "He's awake and conscious," she said crisply, "and still very weak. But he's been asking for you all day, so the doctor suggested we bring you in. Not that I agree totally, but it would seem to make Ryan relax a little more."

"He's awake, Dad, and he wants to see me," I yelled. Soon we were speeding toward the hospital.

Ryan looked so terrible, with gray sunken cheeks, just like my father after his heart attack. I hardly dared speak to him.

"Eden." He croaked my name through cracked lips.

"They wouldn't let me see you before," I said. "I've tried to, but they wouldn't let me in." I crept toward him and took his hand. It was still very hot.

"At least I can feel you touching me now," he said. "I suppose that's a good sign."

He sighed and stared at the ceiling. His blue eyes were as dull as a lake on a cloudy day.

"I've brought something to show you," I said brightly. I got out a newspaper clipping of the show and held it up for him.

"That's nice," he said, hardly even smiling. "Nice to know that once in my life I was famous."

"Oh, come on. Knowing you, you'll be famous at lots of other things. You're a born winner," I said cheerfully, even though my heart was breaking at the sight of him.

"Yeah, maybe needlepoint champion or king

of macramé," he said. "They'll never let me try anything exciting again."

"They might not let you, but I bet you'll find ways to do what you want as soon as you're well again. Do you remember the time we crossed that thin ice and it started to tip and we both got wet legs?"

He nodded. "I remember, but it doesn't seem real any more. The same with the horse jumping. I can't believe that I was up on King just a few days ago."

"King missed you right away," I said. "He kept looking at the gate, waiting for you to come in. When we left without you, he kept looking back, thinking I'd made a mistake."

"Poor King," Ryan said and sighed again. "Nobody lets him do what he wants to do, either. He doesn't belong in a crummy stable. He should be with those other horses up on the hills. He'll never be free. That's why we got on so well. Because we understood each other."

There was a silence. Then, "Will you go on training him now?" he asked. "Will you ride him yourself?"

"I don't know," I said hesitantly. "I'd like to. I don't think I could bear to stay away from him. Old Bradley's talking of selling him, of course. I had a crazy idea that maybe I could enter him in a show myself and persuade Mr. Bradley that King was good advertising for his stable."

"Good luck," he said. "Mr. Bradley's not

exactly known for his heart of gold. I have a feeling if someone waved a bundle of dollar bills at him he would sell his grandmother."

I smiled. "I'm sure you're right," I said. "But until that happens I think I'll keep going. Will you come down and watch me?"

"I don't know," he said. "I can't imagine feeling strong enough to stand up again."

"Sure you will," I said. "You've got to hurry up and get well so we can go on picnics together and have a great summer."

"Eden," Ryan said suddenly and firmly, "I want you to start making more friends. At school, I mean."

"Oh, I'm getting along fine at school now," I said.

Ryan's face frowned in concentration. "No, I don't mean just getting along fine. I mean friends. People that you want to spend time with out of school. You shouldn't just rely on me and the riding stable. One day we might not be there."

"What sort of talk is that?" I said. "You're just feeling down right now because you've got a fever, but you're going to be up and around again soon."

"I guess so," he said. He strained as he took a deep breath, as if the breathing hurt him. "Eden, please stay," he whispered. "I'm going to close my eyes again, but I'd like to know you're here."

"I'll stay as long as they let me," I whispered back. "You just fall asleep, and when you wake up in the morning, I bet you'll feel much better."

"OK," he said as a little boy would. I took his hot hand in mine and sat there, perched uneasily on the edge of that starched, crisp bed. Again I was reminded sharply of my father. I had been terrified he would die then, and now I was even more scared of losing Ryan.

Was that some sort of trial run for me? I wondered. *Was almost losing my dad just preparing me for losing Ryan?*

"Don't die, Ryan," I whispered, looking down at his face, now so peaceful. "Please don't die. I've had to give up so many things I care about already. I don't think I could bear to part with you. You've still got so many things to do. *We've* got so much to do together."

Ryan sighed in his sleep, as if he could sense what I was saying. *I won't let you die,* I thought. *I always used to be a fighter. I almost gave up when we moved away from everything I cared about, but I'm not going to give up anymore. I'm going to keep you going with my own willpower, and I'm going to get you well again.*

"Do you hear me, Ryan?" I said out loud. "You're going to get well again, whether you like it or not!"

Chapter Twenty-three

I don't know if my pep talk did any good, but Ryan really felt a bit better in the morning. The doctors claimed all the credit, saying he was finally responding to the drugs, but I liked to believe that he was getting better for me.

Then suddenly he stopped recovering. Even though the doctors said he was out of danger, I began to get more and more worried about him. His body was recuperating just fine, but he seemed to have lost the will to fight. I often felt as if I were talking to Ryan's ghost. He barely did the exercises for his hand and neck. He would get out of bed and walk around only if he was forced to. He didn't even argue with me anymore.

I dragged myself to school every day and

tried to act like a normal person. Trisha was as good as her word and didn't say anything to anyone else, but she began to invite me to share lunch with her.

"So you've decided we're beneath you now," Renee said, teasing me one day. "You only want to hang around with seniors!"

"No, I don't," I said. "Trisha and I are next-door neighbors."

"OK," Renee said. "Go ahead and desert your friends."

Suddenly I could hear Ryan's voice. "I want you to make friends, Eden." It struck me that we both really needed friends right then. We were both stupid to try to shut out the people who wanted to help us. I'd already begun to realize that things were easier when you shared them.

"I don't want to desert you, Renee," I said seriously. "It's just that I've had this worry on my mind."

"The sick friend you told me about?" she asked.

I nodded.

"Anyone I know?"

I nodded again. "You used to know him. Remember Ryan Benson?"

Her eyes opened wide in amazement. "Ryan Benson? He's the one who's sick?"

I nodded. "Very sick," I said. "I'm so worried about him. He has MS, multiple sclerosis. And he's just had pneumonia and now it's like he's given up. I visit him every day and he just lies there like a log. He's so depressed, and I don't know what to do about it."

She was looking at me with interest. "So it was Ryan all this time?" she asked. "He was the mystery guy you were going with?"

I managed a little grin. "He made me promise I wouldn't let anyone else know why he changed schools," I said.

Renee shook her head. "You mean he left this school just because he didn't want anyone to know he was sick?" she demanded. "How dumb can you get?"

"You know Ryan," I said. "He likes to be the best."

She smiled. "Yeah, that's just the sort of crazy thing he'd do. Do you think we can pop in and visit him sometime?" she asked. "It might cheer him up."

"I don't want to make him mad at me," I said, stopping myself in midthought. "Although, come to think of it, it might be a great idea to make him mad. Anything would be better than having him lie there, thinking that everything's over."

"OK. We'll do it," Renee said. "You let us know when."

"I will," I said. "I'll mention it to him tonight and see what kind of reaction I get. After all, something's got to make him start trying again!"

*   *   *

As I walked up the hospital steps that night and in through the big, pillared front entrance that always scared me a little, I told myself that it was now or never. Somebody had to shake Ryan out of his gloom, and it seemed as if it was up to me. I would tell him about Renee and his friends, make him understand why I went back on my promise, make him understand that he needed friends more than ever now. But it wasn't going to be easy.

Ryan was lying propped up on pillows, staring at a program on TV. Canned laughter floated through the room.

"Hi," he said, barely turning toward me.

"How are you feeling?" I asked, pulling up a chair beside him. "What did the doctors say today?"

"The same," he said in a tired voice. "They always say the same. I'm making progress. I can expect ups and downs from the disease."

"How are you getting along with the tennis ball?" I asked. "Can you crush it yet?"

"What's the point?" Ryan asked with a sigh. "What am I going to do in my life that will involve crushing tennis balls?"

I could see this conversation was rapidly sinking to the level of every other conversation we'd had in the past few days.

"Hey, guess what?" I asked, extra brightly. "How would you like some more visitors tomorrow? I've got a whole bunch of people who want to come to see you."

"Who?" he demanded, eyeing me suspiciously. "What sort of people?"

"Your friends from Evans High," I said.

He attempted to raise himself on the pillows. "You told them about me?" he asked in a horrified voice. "What did you tell them?"

"Everything," I said, trying to sound calm though his face was making me feel scared. "I thought it was about time you realized that you have a lot of things to live for—like a lot of friends, for one thing."

He opened his mouth, but no words came out. His cheeks were as flushed as during the first days of pneumonia.

"You told them all about me?" he asked at last. "You told them about the MS?"

I nodded.

"Eden, how could you do that?" he demanded. "You promised. You broke your promise to me."

"I did it for you, Ryan," I said. "Because I care a lot about you and because you're not getting better. I thought you needed to see that you still have friends."

"I told you I don't want anybody," he said, looking up at the TV set. "I don't want anyone to see me like this and pity me. I just can't believe you'd do this, Eden. I thought you and I loved each other."

"I do love you, Ryan, and I'd do anything to help you get better. But you're wrong about people pitying you. They couldn't believe you'd be so dumb. They couldn't understand that you'd transfer out of school because you were sick. They all want to see you again. They miss you. Can't you get that into your thick skull?"

"Well, I don't want to see them," he said stubbornly. "And I'm not sure that I can forgive you, either."

"In that case," I said, getting up unsteadily, "maybe I'd better go home. I have homework to do, you know."

Ryan's eyes had begun to flash dangerously. "See, I knew it wouldn't last," he said. "I didn't think you'd stick around when I got really sick. I didn't think anybody would. That's why I didn't want any friends."

"You're right," I said. I was almost shouting then, almost crying, too. "I don't know if I want to stick around anymore, because you're not the same person I fell in love with. I thought we were two of a kind, Ryan. We were both fighters, that's what attracted us to each other. But now you've turned into a wimp."

"I'm not a wimp!" he yelled back.

"You sure are," I said. "Just look at yourself, lying there and muttering, 'Poor me, my life is over, I've got nothing worth living for.' I never thought you'd give in like that."

"You try it yourself sometime, Miss-Know-It-All," he shouted. "See just how happy you'd feel if they told you you could never ride again, never do this again, never do that again. Would you feel like going on?"

"I'd be pretty upset, I know that," I said. "I almost didn't feel like going on when Dad had his heart attack and we had to move. But you know what I found? There are lots of sweet things in life, Ryan, even if you can't ride anymore, even if you have to sit in a wheelchair someday."

Ryan's head was still turned away from me, staring up at the TV set from which great shrieks of laughter were coming.

"I'm going now," I said. "I don't think you and I have anything more to say to each other right now." I walked toward the door and turned to look back at him. "You have to decide for yourself that life is worth living. Nobody else can decide that for you."

I was shaking as I ran down the hall. *Have I done the right thing?* I worried. I remembered that stress can bring on acute attacks with MS. What if I was responsible for a terrible relapse in Ryan? What if his mother decided I was bad news and wouldn't let me see him again? What if the pneumonia came back and this time he didn't get over it?

As the evening wore on, another worry crept in to mingle with these. What if he didn't want to see me anymore?

That night I had a terrible nightmare that his mother came and wheeled him away during the night, and when I went to the hospital the next morning, all I saw was an empty bed and no one knew where he had gone. I wondered if I should go to the hospital as usual the next evening or if it would be better if I stayed away.

But I'd hardly woken up the next morning when the phone rang.

"Eden?" a voice asked cautiously.

"Ryan?"

"Hi."

"Hi."

"Eden, I'm sorry about last night."

"I am, too. I shouldn't have upset you."

"You were doing what you thought was best for me, I know that now."

"I want you to get better, Ryan. That's all."

"I know. Will you come this evening as usual?"

"Of course I will."

"That's good. 'Bye, Eden."

" 'Bye, Ryan."

That evening when I went to the hospital, it was as if somebody had opened the drapes and let in the sunshine. Ryan was sitting up in bed, frowning with concentration while he squeezed a tennis ball in his right hand.

"Stupid ball," he muttered, looking up as I came in. "I think it's made of concrete."

"But you can squeeze," I said. "That's terrific."

"I've been lying around here too long," he said. "I'm getting bored with the same old nurses. But they won't let me out until I can squeeze stupid tennis balls and do all sorts of dumb things."

He looked up and smiled. His face was different. His eyes had a sparkle in them again. It was only a faint sparkle of light blue, but it was definitely there. "You look like Rip Van Winkle after his long sleep," I said.

"I do not," he answered. "Hey, I just squeezed the tennis ball out of my hand again."

I bent to retrieve it as it bounced across the room. "They'll be mad if you knock over their equipment," I said.

"Serve them right. They're a bunch of bullies," he said. "I've made up my mind that once I get out of here, I'm never coming back into a hospital again!"

"What happened to you?" I asked. "Last night you were prepared to lie here forever."

"You were right, Eden," he said. "I hate to admit this but you were right. After you'd gone last night, I wondered what would happen if you never came back. And I tried to imagine life without you. I couldn't do it, Eden. I'm glad you're stubborn and you've got a big mouth! You can help me get out of this place."

"I'm sorry I broke that promise, but it was a dumb promise," I said. "You can't shut yourself off from other people, because you need other people to keep you going. I should know. I tried it, and it was the worst time in my life. I've only kept going through these past few days because of other people, Ryan. My dad and my friends at school. Renee's dying to see you again, although I forbid you to notice that she's prettier than me!"

Ryan laughed. "You are funny," he said. "And she's not prettier than you. You really think I should see her?"

"I really think you should," I said.

"I was wondering," Ryan said hesitantly, "about something else, too. I should write to my father. After all, I'm still his son, and even if he doesn't want to live with us anymore, he may still want to keep in touch."

He reached over and took my hand. It was wonderful to feel his hand on mine again, his warm fingers curling around mine once again. "Isn't that what you're trying to say it's all about?" he continued. "A whole long line of people, all reaching out toward one another, all making a chain and keeping in touch?"

"I'm sure of it, Ryan," I said. "We all want to be part of your life if you'll only let us in."

From that day on Ryan was a terrible patient. Renee and I got a gang of his old friends from Evans together, and we almost got kicked out of the hospital when we descended on Ryan's room. Then he disobeyed rules and bugged the staff so much that they couldn't wait to see him go. He made a fuss about taking pills and naps and used equipment he wasn't supposed to in the physiotherapy room.

"Hey, guess what?" he said on the day he checked out. "The doctors have said I've got to take up swimming as therapy. I used to be on a swim team when I was eight. I was pretty hot stuff at the butterfly, I remember." He started waving his arms about wildly, doing

219

a good imitation of the butterfly stroke. He knocked over his water jug and started laughing.

"Oh, yes," I said, helping mop up the water with his towel. "Very impressive. Only I think you'd go faster in deeper water!"

"Very funny," he said. "You wait till I'm the next Olympic butterfly champ."

"I can see a stay in the hospital hasn't done anything to deflate your ego," I said, laughing.

"Well, you have to aim high, don't you," he said, laughing, too. "I can't see me as one of those old ladies who do sidestrokes up and down the pool. I think I can keep going as long as I have somewhere to go."

"Knowing you," I said, "you'll probably turn out to be the world's greatest butterflyer. It's very sickening the way you can do everything."

Chapter Twenty-four

I didn't get down to the stables as much as I should have during the next couple of weeks. One of the reasons was that I was practicing to get my driver's license. I couldn't keep asking Dad to take me to Ryan's as often as I wanted to go. And Ryan needed me. He was having a hard time settling in at home. It was very frustrating for him to be back in his old surroundings and not be allowed to do things.

His mother hovered over him like a mother hen, clucking every time he tried to do things for himself. She and I were getting on a little better. At least she realized I had been helpful in getting Ryan over his crisis, but she always watched me suspiciously, as if she were sure I'd force him onto a horse again the moment her back was turned.

"So how is King doing?" he asked one evening when I had shown up late. It was the first time he'd mentioned the horse since he came home. "Are you still taking him over the course pretty often?"

"Not often," I replied, playing with the fringe of one of the pillows and not looking up at him. "There doesn't seem to be any point. It's only a matter of time before Bradley sells him."

Ryan came over to me. "Poor Eden," he said, putting his hand on mine. "It hardly seems fair, does it? First you have to give up one horse, then you find another, even better one, and have to give him up, too. I wonder how much he wants for King? I've got to sell my motorbike, you know."

I looked up at him, understanding what he was thinking. For a second a wild surge of hope flashed through me: Ryan wanted to buy the horse for me! Then I managed to stop thinking of myself and wondered what it would do to Ryan, owning a horse that he could never ride again. Wouldn't it hurt him to watch me ride King all the time? Wouldn't he be reminded every day of his limitations and his own helplessness? Wouldn't he be tempted to try it just once more?

I remembered that I hadn't really understood when my mother insisted we give up the ranch. She didn't want Dad to have to sit back and watch other people do his job. Now

I knew that I could never put Ryan through that kind of heartache, either, even if it meant giving up the most wonderful horse I'd ever ridden.

"I couldn't let you do that," I told him.

"Why not," he demanded, a spark of his old fire lighting his eyes. "I thought you were the one who said that people should help each other. I want to do so much for you, Eden."

"But not this, Ryan," I said. "It wouldn't work. For one thing, your mother wouldn't let you own a horse you weren't allowed to ride."

"So I wouldn't tell her," he said. "I bought the motorbike with my own money."

"You're crazy," I said, smiling at him and squeezing his hand. "Like I said once to my father, maybe it's time I gave up horses and concentrated on boys!"

"But you really like that horse, Eden," Ryan protested.

"So do you," I said gently. "We'll learn to let him go together."

Every day at the stables I groomed King extra carefully, brushing his flanks until they shone like gold and combing out his mane until it lay in my hand like spun silver. It was as if I wanted to imprint every detail about him on my mind.

Even Mr. Bradley noticed all the extra care King was getting.

"You're really doing a good job with that

horse," he commented as he shuffled past me. "I reckon he'll bring me top dollar at the sale, and it's all thanks to you."

"Sale?" I asked. "What sale?"

"The one over in Waverly on Saturday. I'm going to put him in. I can't wait to watch them all trying to outbid each other to get him!"

"But you won't even know the person who buys him that way," I said. "You won't know if he'll be going to a good home."

"You get more for a horse in a good auction," Mr. Bradley said, looking at me as if I were stupid. "A lot of rich folks will be there, and he's a flashy-looking horse. Just so long as the buyer has cash in his hand, he can be Count Dracula for all I care!"

I pretended to be busy with getting a tangle out of King's mane, because I didn't want Mr. Bradley to see my anger.

"You know," he went on, tactless as usual, "you deserve the credit for this horse. If it hadn't been for you, he could have ended up as dog meat. Don't think I'm not grateful. If he gets what I hope he'll get at the sale, I'll give you a hundred dollars. How about that, eh?"

Something snapped inside me as he said that. I looked up at him. He stood there, looking extra pleased with himself, grinning his horrible black-toothed grin. The man really thought he was being so wonderful!

"Money! That's all you care about, isn't it?"

I yelled, unable to control myself any longer. "That's all that matters to you. It never entered your head that it might be breaking my heart to part with this horse. I don't think you've even noticed how much I care about him. I've worked with him, trained him into a terrific jumper, and now I'm never going to see him again. You think a hundred dollars will make everything all right?"

The words just spilled out in a jumble. I didn't want Mr. Bradley to see me crying, so I pushed past him and ran out of the stall, with the curry comb still in my hand. My feet clattered over the cement of the stable yard. I pushed open the tack room door and ran inside, seeking sanctuary in its darkness. I had to get away from there, far away from the horrible old man and his broken-down stable yard. The moment King was gone, I was going, too, and never coming back again. There were other riding schools in the city. I'd get a summer job somewhere bigger and better, maybe at a stable with an indoor ring! Maybe I'd train lots of horses for English jumping competitions. After all, not many horses would be a challenge after King!

I wondered who would buy him. Would they be able to do what Ryan had done? Maybe King would become a famous horse, and I'd be able to watch him on TV and know that it was all thanks to us. But what if somebody horrible bought him? Or, worst of all, a fancy riding school where he would just plod in a line with the other horses, a new person on his back every weekend. Then if he ever showed his spirit, he'd be sold again, passed along from one person who couldn't control him to the next.

I stood alone in the darkness of the tack room. The strong smell of leather and polish and horse sweat was all around me. I was sweating, too, because I'd just had a crazy idea. I wouldn't let Mr. Bradley sell King. I'd take him back up to the hills and set him free where he belonged. I would get into terrible trouble, but it would be worth it. I owed it to King!

My hands were trembling as I came out of the tack room and went back to my work. Mr. Bradley avoided me, knowing what my bad moods could be like. I pretended to be hard at work every time he shuffled past me, and I kept on praying that he would go home and leave the locking up to me.

It was almost dark when he finally appeared behind me.

"Still working?" he grunted. "I'm going home. Make sure you lock everything up well, won't you?"

"OK," I said, not looking up. I heard his feet disappearing down the stable yard. I heard the gate creak and the latch slam back into place. Then I ran back into the tack room and brought out King's halter.

King looked at me in surprise as I slid it onto his head.

"Why are we going out when it's almost dark?" his eyes asked me clearly. Those eyes looked at me suspiciously, as if he could sense my tension.

"Don't worry, old man," I whispered to him. 'I'm going to give you what you want most. I'm going to set you free. Ryan will never be free again, and I'll never go back to where I was happiest, but at least you can be free. You can run over the hills and think of us stuck down here in the city.

"Come on, King," I said, opening his stall and leading him out. His feet made such a loud clatter, echoing across the stable yard, that I expected Mr. Bradley to come running back to see what was wrong. But we reached the gate and found the street outside deserted. Bradley's old truck and trailer were parked in the rickety garage beside the yard. I wasn't at all sure that I could drive the truck, but at least I had my license now. I opened the lock on the garage door. It swung open with a rusty squeak that set King dancing nervously.

"Easy, old fellow," I whispered, running my hand down his smooth, warm flank. I slipped the leading rein around the door handle while I went inside to open the trailer. Like everything else on the Bradley property, the trailer was so old it was almost falling to pieces. I wrestled with the rusty bolt that held its door in place. It wouldn't move. I wrapped an old piece of burlap around my hand and tried again.

"Come on," I pleaded angrily. "Open!" The bolt wouldn't even wiggle. I picked up a rock and pounded at it again.

"Open!" I yelled. "Come on, open!" It seemed so unfair that my wonderful plan could be foiled because of one rusty bolt.

"Eden?" A voice behind me startled me. I dropped the rock.

I spun around. "Ryan? What are you doing here?"

"That's what I call a real friendly greeting," he said as he approached. "I stopped by your house and you weren't home. I figured you might be here."

"But you're not supposed to be driving yet," I said, torn between delight at having him there beside me and knowing that he was doing more than he should.

His face broke into a big grin. "I went for my check-up today," he said. "And the doctor told me I could drive if I took it easy and just cruised around."

"That's great, Ryan," I said, managing a smile. "Now maybe you can help me."

"What are you doing in there, anyway?" he asked. "And why is King out? It's almost dark!"

"I'm setting him free, Ryan," I said excitedly.

"You're what?" he demanded.

"Old Bradley's going to sell him on Saturday. I don't want him to go to just anybody, so I decided to take him back to the hills where he belongs. But I couldn't open the stupid bolt on the trailer, and I'm so glad you're here because now you can help me get King in—"

"Eden," Ryan interrupted, "have you lost your mind? You can't take King like that. It's stealing."

"But, Ryan, he's going to be sold. Maybe somebody terrible will buy him. I can't let that happen, Ryan. I love him too much." I was really crying now, not just odd tears trickling down my cheek but a great torrent of tears, spilling out of my eyes and wetting my chin.

Ryan tried to take me in his arms. "I know it's hard for you," he said gently, "but you can't do this. It's wrong. You'd just get in big trouble."

"I don't care," I said, pushing him away. "If you really loved me, and you really cared about King, you'd want to help, not just stand there telling me I'm being stupid."

"Well, you *are* being stupid," he snapped. "Do you want to end up in juvenile court?"

"You don't really care at all," I yelled, pushing past him to begin wrestling the bolt again. "If you don't want to help, then get out of here. I don't want to make you an accessory to the crime!"

"I'm not going to let you do it," Ryan said, grabbing at me.

"Let go of me!" I screamed, fighting his strong arms.

"Eden, calm down, will you? Just listen to me for a minute," he said in a gentle voice.

His hold was so tight I couldn't move. In the end I gave up struggling and collapsed against him like a rag doll.

"Ryan, I only want to help King," I said. "I'd never forgive myself if he went to a miserable life."

"I know," he said. "I feel the same way, but that's no reason to steal him and let him go in the hills."

"But you were the one who said he'd never be free again!" I gulped back a sob.

"Apart from the fact that King is not yours to set free, you might not even be doing him a favor," Ryan said.

"What do you mean?" I asked. "Don't you think he'd want to be with the wild horses again?"

"He might," Ryan said. "But they might reject him because he's been around humans for so long. He's broken now, remember? He might not be able to survive in the wild anymore."

"You really think so?" I asked in a small voice.

"I'm no expert," he said. "But it seems possible, doesn't it?"

I nodded against his shoulder.

"You are crazy sometimes," Ryan said, stroking my hair. "Maybe that's why I love you."

"But what can we do about King?" I whispered. "Old Bradley doesn't care who he sells him to, as long as they pay cash."

We hope you enjoyed reading this book. If you would like to receive
further information about titles available in the Bantam series, just write
to the address below, with your name and address: Kim Prior, Bantam
Books, 61–63 Uxbridge Road, Ealing, London W5 5SA.

If you live in Australia or New Zealand and would like more information
about the series, please write to:

Sally Porter
Transworld Publishers (Aust) Pty
Ltd.
15-23 Helles Avenue
Moorebank
N.S.W. 2170
AUSTRALIA

Kiri Martin
Transworld Publishers (NZ) Ltd
Cnr. Moselle and Waipareira
Avenues
Henderson
Auckland
NEW ZEALAND

All Bantam Young Adult books are available at your bookshop or news-
agent, or can be ordered from the following address: Corgi/Bantam
Books, Cash Sales Department, PO Box 11, Falmouth, Cornwall, TR10
9EN.

Please list the title(s) you would like, and send together with a cheque
or postal order. You should allow for the cost of the book(s) plus postage
and packing charges as follows:

All orders up to a total of £5.00: 50p
All orders in excess of £5.00: Free

Please note that payment must be made in pounds sterling; other
currencies are unacceptable.

(The above applies to readers in the UK and Republic of Ireland only)

B.F.P.O. customers, please allow for the cost of the book(s) plus the
following for postage and packing: 60p for the first book, 25p for the
second book and 15p per copy for the next 7 books, thereafter 9p per
book.

Overseas customers, please allow £1.25 for postage and packing for
the first book, 75p for the second book, and 28p for each subsequent
title ordered.

Thank you!

All That Glitters

It's the New Hit Series from
Bantam Books that takes you behind
the scenes of a T.V. Soap Opera.

Share the highs and lows, the hits and flops, the glamour
and hard work, the glory and heartache of life on the

Soap Set with:

KATIE	SHANA	MITCH
NOLAN	BRADBURY	CALLAHAN

Each a star in their own right, each a seasoned
professional aiming for the top, each a teenager dealing
with the ups and downs, the crazy ins and outs of teenage
life—all in the glaring light of the camera's all-seeing eye!

ALL THAT GLITTERS
It's Golden

Janet Quin-Harkin's Sugar & Spice

Watch out for a smashing new series from the best-selling author, Janet Quin-Harkin.

Meet the most unlikely pair of best friends since Toni and Jill from Janet Quin-Harkin's TEN BOY SUMMER.

Caroline's thrilled to find out she's got a long-lost cousin exactly her age. But she's horrified when Chrissy comes to spend a year with her family. Caroline's a reserved and polite only child — now she has to share her life with a loud, unsophisticated, embarrassing farm girl!

Coming soon — wherever Bantam paperbacks are sold!